SEA GIRL

FEMINIST FOLKTALES FROM AROUND THE WORLD | Vol. III

ETHEL JOHNSTON PHELPS

Introduction by DANIEL JOSÉ OLDER
With illustrations by SUKI BOYNTON

For a future hero! xx Suki

FP **FEMINIST PRESS** AT THE CITY UNIVERSITY OF NEW YORK NEW YORK CITY

Published in 2017 by the Feminist Press
at the City University of New York
The Graduate Center
365 Fifth Avenue, Suite 5406
New York, NY 10016

feministpress.org

First Feminist Press edition 2017

This book was made possible thanks to a grant from New York State Council
on the Arts with the support of Governor Andrew Cuomo and the New York
State Legislature.

First printing August 2017

Cover and text design by Suki Boynton

Library of Congress Cataloging-in-Publication Data is available for this title.

*To Carol Levin and Ranice Crosby
for more reasons than I could ever list*

CONTENTS

INTRODUCTION

DANIEL JOSÉ OLDER

We need a new mythology.

We—writers, thinkers, readers, revolutionaries—shout it over and over; we yell it from the rooftops and write it in the sky. The stories that made it through the power sieve of history so rarely do justice to our multilayered, incendiary existences, our many faces, our struggles. There's a reason for that, and it's one that we lay bare again and again with our counternarratives as we fight for a truer, more equitable literature, a new mythology.

But what about the stories that didn't make it through? What about those way-back-when literary rebellions? Those apocryphal folktales that various hierarchies and Disney didn't deem "marketable" or whatever popular excuse was used to justify keeping the powerful comfortable. After all, before Suzanne

Collins wrote Katniss Everdeen or Octavia Butler wrote Lauren Olamina or Nalo Hopkinson wrote Tan-Tan or I wrote Sierra Santiago, someone, long, long ago, wrote the Summer Queen and the Maid of the North and Sea Girl.

As a kid, I adored Greek and Roman mythology. All these tiny, gigantic stories wove together to form this incredible, multilayered universe. The gods were as flawed and fascinating as the mortals, and all the love and war that ensued seemed to go on forever—a book that never begins and never ends. "Eros and Psyche" was one of my favorites, it still is, but, like so many myths, the "Eros and Psyche" I read over and over again as a kid was wildly different than the earlier version. In the children's version—the popular, acceptable one—Psyche, a guest in the mysterious castle of her mysterious, hidden husband, breaks the trust of their marriage by lighting a candle late at night to see what he really looks like. The light reveals Eros as the god he really is and a single drop of wax burns him. The spell is broken. The story wraps up pretty quickly after that: depending on the version, some political wrangling happens and they either live happily ever after or not—cool.

But one day, out of curiosity, I looked up one of the first recorded versions. It's in a book called *The*

Golden Ass by a fellow named Apuleius who lived in an Ancient Roman colony in what is now Algeria. I have a very elegant, tattered copy that I found at the Brattle Book Shop in Boston, but it looks like it could've come right out of Hogwarts. This Psyche isn't defined by her single act of distrust. She is complex, she has a community around her—concerned parents and a sister who plants the seeds of doubt. More than that, she is determined, tenacious, in love. The whole mess with the candle happens halfway through Apuleius's story, not at the end. After that, Eros withdraws to the overprotective embrace of his vengeful mom, Aphrodite, who sends her minions after Psyche. And Psyche, pregnant, alone, eternally badass, and still very human, goes on the run. She traverses heaven and earth, journeys into the bowels of hell, and seeks alliances with the spirits of the world. In short, she sets out on her own hero's quest, finally walking straight into the lair of her own tormentor, at the summit of Olympus, and facing her head on.

I think my mouth must've fallen open when I first read that. *Where was this story when I was a kid??*

In the book you're holding, you'll find a Scandinavian version of the Eros and Psyche myth, "East of the Sun, West of the Moon." In it, the protagonist sets out on a perilous mission to save her enchanted husband. She allies with the wind and journeys to the land of trolls. Over and over again, she says: "I am not afraid."

Also in these pages, you'll meet Gina the young giant, who reaches out to bridge the gap between her people and the nearby villagers, changing the course of history; and the Summer Queen, who faces off with the fearsome Winter Giant to save the lands of the North. You'll read about Sea Girl, who daringly sneaks into the Dragon King's lair to help her people. Here, as in life, the women and girls of the world are heroes, overcoming tremendous obstacles for the benefit of their communities and the people they love.

"We have always fought," Kameron Hurley wrote in her award-winning essay of the same name. But history has swallowed up the narratives of so many of those fights, the multifaceted story of those moments of women's empowerment, those toppled patriarchies. That pointed and damaging erasure requires us, in our journeys toward this new mythology, to also have an eye toward the past. It means we must become heroic archeologists, as Alice Walker was for Zora Neale Hurston, and muddle through the shattered remnants left in the wake of the ongoing march of the powerful. "There's nothing new under the sun," Octavia

Butler told us, "but there are new suns." Within these pages you will discover that there are also very old suns, long hidden and thought lost, and long overdue for some shine.

PREFACE

ETHEL JOHNSTON PHELPS

The traditional fairy and folktales in this collection, as in my earlier books of tales, have one characteristic in common: they all portray spirited, courageous heroines. Although a great number of such collections are in print, this type of heroine is surprisingly rare.

Taken as a whole, the body of traditional fairy and folktales (the two terms have become almost interchangeable) is very heavily weighted with heroes, and most of the "heroines" we do encounter are far from heroic. Always endowed with beauty—and it often appears that beauty is their only reason for being in the tale—they conform in many ways to the sentimental ideal of women in the nineteenth century. They are good, obedient, meek, submissive to authority, and naturally inferior to the heroes. They sometimes suffer cruelties, but are patient under ill treatment. In most cases they are docile or helpless when confronted with danger or a difficult situation.

In short, as heroines, they do not inspire or delight, but tend to bore the reader. I think it is their meekness that repels. They are acted upon by people or events in the tale; they rarely initiate their own action to change matters. (In contrast to this type of heroine, when clever or strong women appear in folktales, they are usually portrayed as unpleasant, if not evil, characters—cruel witches, jealous stepmothers, or old hags.) It is not my intention to delve into the psychological or social meanings behind the various images of heroines in folktales, but simply to note that the vast majority are not particularly satisfying to readers today.

In actual fact, the women of much earlier centuries, particularly rural women, were strong, capable, and resourceful in a positive way, as hardworking members of a family or as widows on their own. Few folktales reflect these qualities. Inevitably the question arises: How many, if any, folktales of strong, capable heroines exist in the printed sources available?

In a sense, this book grew out of that question. Over a period of three years I read thousands of fairy and folktales in search for tales of clever, resourceful heroines; tales in which equally courageous heroines and heroes cooperated in their adventures; tales of likable heroines who had the spirit to take action; tales that were, in themselves, strong or appealing.

As a result of that search, the heroines in this book are quite different from the usual folk- and fairy-tale heroines. In a few of the tales, the girls and women possess the power (or knowledge) of magic, which they use to rescue the heroes from disaster. The hero may be more physically active in the story, but he needs the powers of the self-reliant, independent heroine to save him.

In the majority of the tales, the heroines are resourceful girls and women who take action to solve a problem posed by the plot. Often they use cleverness or shrewd common sense.

All the heroines have self-confidence and a clear sense of their own worth. They possess courage, moral or physical; they do not meekly accept but seek to solve the dilemmas they face. The majority have leading roles in the story. However, the few with minor roles (in terms of space) play a crucial part in the story and have an independent strength characteristic of all the heroines here.

Although most of the printed sources for the tales I've chosen are from the nineteenth century, the tales themselves are part of an oral, primarily rural tradition of storytelling that stretches far back in time. Each generation shaped the tales according to the values of the time, adding or subtracting details according to the teller's own sense of story. While the characters and basic story remained the same, it was this personal shaping of the tales that may explain the many variations of each story that now exist. As every folktale reader knows, different versions of the tales are found in different countries and even on different continents. Variants of Cinderella and of tales of hero/heroines bewitched into nonhuman form are particularly widespread.

In giving the older tales of our heritage a fresh retelling for this generation of readers, I have exercised the traditional storyteller's privilege. I have shaped each tale, sometimes adding or omitting details, to reflect my sense of what makes it a satisfying tale. "The Maid of the North," for example, has been compressed to make a smoother flow of narrative.

Most of the tales in this book follow the story outlines of earlier sources quite closely. In a few cases I've added my own details to amplify the story's ending, as in "The Giant's Daughter."

The tale "Fair Exchange" is retold with the most freedom. Of the many tales of changelings in Celtic folklore, none caught my imagination for retelling.

The story of the lass in "Fair Exchange" springs from a brief incident in one of Lady Wilde's tales of Irish folklore. I developed the incident of the girl who confronted the Fairy Queen to get her own child back into the present story, blending elements of other folktales to fill in the details.

For the tale "Gawain and the Lady Ragnell," I have used the versions from fourteenth-century literary storytellers who drew on oral folktales of their period as sources. As might be expected, this is more complex than other tales in the collection. However, there are tales to appeal to the very young as well as the more sophisticated reader. Through the tales' diversity, the reader becomes aware of the extraordinary vitality of the fairy and folktale heritage, not only in the range of imaginative fantasy but also in humor.

I confess a partiality for the lighthearted tale. There is sly humor in the chaos caused by the powerful Gina in "The Giant's Daughter." In the Punjab story of the clever wife, "The Tiger and the Jackal," it is the two animals who provide the humor. A sense of the comic pervades "The Monkey's Heart," where a small monkey uses her wit to get rid of a shark. Even "The Maid of the North," a tale from the heroic saga known as the *Kalevala*, contains a clear thread of skeptical humor.

Two of the tales in the book deserve longer

comment. The basic fairy tale plot of "Gawain and the Lady Ragnell" was old in Chaucer's day (as the Wife of Bath remarked when she told a variant of the tale). By the late fourteenth century the tale had become attached to King Arthur and Gawain, in the sense that they were given the leading male roles in the story. Of all the northern tales told about Arthur and Gawain, this one is the tenderest and most appealing. It will be noticed that the King Arthur and Gawain of northern British folklore are quite different from the same characters in T. H. White's *The Once and Future King* or Thomas Malory's *Le Morte d'Arthur*, drawn from French sources. To the storytellers in the north of Britain, Gawain was the ideal of a hero, Arthur was flawed with human failings, and Lancelot was a minor knight rarely mentioned. These northern tales of Arthur lack the high romance of the French tales, but their dry humor and ironic realism are very engaging.

This is a tale of shape-changing and evil enchantment. Ragnell faces her terrible situation with courage, saves Arthur's life, and finds in Gawain a man with the necessary personal qualities to help her break the enchantment.

The underlying theme of a woman's right to freedom of will and choice weaves the different story elements together. The woman who "wanted her own way" was often made fun of in folktales, for it is an issue as old as human relationships. It's refreshing to find that a few tales do handle the theme in positive terms—and delightful to find the theme used as a basis for a romantic story.

"The Maid of the North," the longest story in the book, is drawn from the Finnish saga, the *Kalevala*. Kalevala is known as the Land of Heroes, and the saga deals primarily with the heroes' adventures, feuds, and journeys to the North Land. However, woven through the songs and tales in the saga like a bright thread is the story of the Maid and her mother, Louhi. I have pulled out the incidents dealing with the Maid of the North in order to tell her story as a separate tale.

All the women in the *Kalevala* have strong, independent characters. This particular tale is concerned with Louhi, the ruler of the North Land, and her daughter, the Maid—who, as is often the case in folktales, is not given a specific name. Although the women and the heroes in the tale have supernatural powers, these powers are limited; they often land in predicaments from which their powers cannot extricate them.

The heroes from Kalevala have magic in powerful word and song charms; the two women from the North Land have lesser and quite different powers of magic. Both the heroes and the women rely on guile rather than physical force. Although in this retelling it was necessary to compress the heroes' adventures, they are without doubt the most energetic characters in the tale, and the women from the North Land regard them with mocking amusement.

Of the three very different heroes who seek to marry the Maid, she finally chooses young Seppo the smith. Given three impossible tasks to perform, Seppo turns to the Maid for help; the Maid's clever counsel enables him to accomplish the "impossible" and saves his life.

The charm of the tale lies in the humorous vitality of the characters. Despite their prodigious deeds and powers, the heroes (in fact, all the characters) are engagingly human in their frailties.

Although I have taken the greater part of this introduction to speak of the remarkably spirited heroines I have culled from the large body of traditional folktales, I cannot end without a few words about the heroes who appear in some of the tales with them. By and large, they are not the stereotyped heroes of most fairy and folktales. They are not flat, cardboard characters, but are individually appealing in their own right: Prince Wilhelm in despair over dual promises; the compassionate, incomparable Gawain; and the shy master smith, Seppo, who wins the heart of the Maid of the North.

But enough has been said about the quite special heroines—and heroes—in these tales. The proof is in the reading.

The MAID of the NORTH

ong, long ago Finland was called Kalevala, the Land of Heroes, for the people who lived there possessed magic in the power of words. They could sing a word-spell strong enough to heal mortal wounds, raise a golden pine tree, or even challenge the power of Hiisi the Evil One. In the cold, snowy land to the north dwelled a very different folk, and the most powerful of these were the Mistress of the North Country, old Louhi, and her daughter, the Maid of the North.

Early one morning, after Louhi's farmhouse had been swept and scoured, a young serving girl came out into the yard to empty a pan of scraps. Hearing a strange sound from across the river, she stopped to listen, then ran back into the house.

"Someone is in trouble across the river, Mistress," she cried. "It sounds like a child weeping."

Old Louhi came out and crossed the yard to peer through the gates. On the distant, marshy shore of the river, she could barely make out the form of a man, but she could clearly hear his despairing laments. "That's not a child weeping," she remarked. "It's more likely the wild moaning of a hero in trouble!"

Louhi hurried down to untie the boat moored at the river's edge. Then she rowed across the wide river to the place on the bleak shore where a gray-bearded man was standing.

"Who are you, stranger?" called Louhi as she came near to him. "Where do you come from?"

"I come from the South—from Kalevala, the Land of Heroes, and I am a great man in my own country," he answered. "But I've met with terrible misfortune, and now I'm completely lost in this strange, bleak country." He added bitterly, "I should have stayed at home!"

"Come out of that soggy marsh and get into my boat," said Louhi briskly. "I'll bring you back to my farmstead, and you can tell me all about your troubles."

The shivering old man climbed gratefully into the boat. Louhi, with strong strokes of the oars, sent the small craft skimming back across the river. Then she fed him, warmed him before the fire, and dried his wet clothes.

"I am Väinämöinen," he said when he was dry and comfortable. "In Kalevala, I am known as a singer of powerful songs."

Louhi nodded. She had heard of Väinämöinen and his powers of magic. "And what brings you to the North, Väinä? Why did you leave the rich green fields and sunny lakes of the South?"

He sighed. "I am a foolish old man. I decided it was time I was married, and I thought to find a wife in the North Country." Then he related the troubles and misfortunes that had befallen him on his way north. "And finally," he concluded, "when I was thrown into the sea, I swam desperately for days until an eagle from Lapland took pity on me, swooped down, and carried me off on his back. He dropped me there on the marsh." He shivered. "It is a cold, gloomy country. I want nothing more than to leave it and return to my own land."

Louhi regarded him thoughtfully. He was, she knew, a magician of great power—deposited, so to speak, on her own doorstep. It was possible he could be of use to her.

"Stop your lamenting, Väinä," she said kindly. "You have come to a good country. You could live here in comfort. There is honey mead to drink, plenty of salmon on the table, and pork—"

"I don't care for strange food in strange houses," he said crossly. "A man is better off at home, where his power and dignity are known. I am too old to search for a wife."

"If that's the case," said Louhi craftily, "what will you give me if I send you back to the green fields of your own land?"

"Whatever you like!" said old Väinä eagerly. "A hat full of silver and gold? Two hats full?"

"Gold and silver are not of much use to me," said Louhi, "and I have copper in the Copper Mountain yonder. But life is not very easy here in the cold North Land. The one thing I want is a magic Sampo—a mill that grinds out flour and meal on one side, salt on the other, and coins on the third side. If you could make me a magic Sampo, I'd give you a horse and sledge to carry you home in comfort!"

When Väinämöinen did not answer, Louhi went on, "I have the white swan's plume needed for its making, but where is the hero who can forge the Sampo?"

Väinä knew he had no power to forge a Sampo. He said cautiously, "I've heard of such a thing, but nothing like that exists in all the land."

"I have a handsome daughter, the Maid of the North," Louhi added slyly. "I will give my daughter in marriage to whoever will make me a magic Sampo."

Väinä's eyes lit up for a moment. Then he said regretfully, "I cannot make you a Sampo. But I do

6

know a man who can—Seppo Ilmarinen the Master Smith. He is the greatest smith in the Land of Heroes. It was he who forged the dome of the sky. You see how smooth it is—not a hammer mark on it! If you send me back to my own country, I promise that Ilmarinen will come to the North Land to forge you the magic Sampo."

"Agreed," said Louhi. She thought Ilmarinen would be just the man for the work. She harnessed a horse to the sledge, settled fur rugs around old Väinä, and gave him cold salmon and eggs for provisions.

"The horse will take you south swiftly and safely. He knows the way. But I have one word of warning for you," said Louhi. "Do not lift your head to look upward or around you until you arrive in Kalevala. If you do, misfortune will follow."

Väinä thanked her for her kindness and drove off. His head sunk in thought, he considered how he was going to persuade his friend Ilmarinen to go to the North Country.

Väinämöinen had traveled only a short distance on his journey when he heard a sharp, clicking clatter of sound. What could it be? He looked about him. There was nothing in sight but snow and distant forests of pine and spruce. Forgetting Louhi's warning, he lifted his head and looked upward.

He stared in amazement. Quite close above him

in the gray, northern sky was the arc of a rainbow. On the rainbow sat a dazzling young woman weaving at a loom. There was only one young woman who could sit on a rainbow—with a loom or without—and that was powerful old Louhi's daughter, the Maid of the North.

"So this is why the old sorceress forbade me to lift my head!" thought Väinä. "She did not want me to elope with the Maid of the North before she gets her Sampo!"

The girl on the rainbow was laughing at him. Väinä remembered he had been seeking a wife, and thought this dark-haired charmer would do very well.

"Climb down, Maid of the North, and sit beside me in the sledge," he called.

"Why should I do that?" she asked in amusement.

"I will take you home with me to the fair South Land. You can bake bread for me, brew my beer, and talk to me gaily when I come home in the evenings."

Her laughter rang out. "Yesterday I heard a bird singing of marriage. I asked him if a woman was happier in her own house or in the home of a husband. Do you know what he answered? 'A maiden's lot is brighter than a day in summer, but a married woman's lot is colder than frost. A girl at home is as free as a berry in a garden, but a wife is like a house dog tied with a rope.' Why should I be a servant and wait upon a husband?"

"The bird knows nothing about it!" Väinä answered irritably. "Every girl should get married! I will not make a bad husband. I am no lazier than other heroes."

The Maid laughed again at Väinä's words. "I'll think about it—if you will split a horsehair with a knife and tie an egg into knots without breaking the shell!" she mocked.

Väinä smiled and climbed out of the sledge. "That's nothing for a hero from Kalevala!" He plucked a hair from the horse's mane. Taking a knife from his belt, he split the hair cleanly into pieces so thin one could scarcely see them. Then he took an egg Louhi had given him and tied it into knots without even cracking the shell.

"Now will you come and sit in the sledge with me?" he called.

"Perhaps," said the Maid. "Let me see you peel a stone and chop a block of ice without scattering any chips."

Väinä peeled a stone as neatly as an apple and chopped the ice fine, without spilling a chip.

"There!" said Väinä, very pleased with himself. "Now will you come down to the sledge?"

"Very clever," admitted the Maid. Then, with

a grin of mischief, she said, "I might come down if you make me a boat from the wooden pieces of my loom, and launch the boat without touching it!" She tossed the loom down to him and sat back to watch.

"There is no man in the world who can build boats better than I can!" boasted Väinä. Taking his ax from the sledge, he set to work. Hour after hour he worked—until a downward blow of the ax slipped and cut deep into his knee. He hopped about in agony, the blood gushing from the wound. Too late, he remembered Louhi's warning of misfortune. He looked upward, but both the Maid and the rainbow had vanished.

He sang all the healing spells he could think of; he gathered moss and lichen for poultices, but nothing stopped the flow of blood. He had once known of a special magic spell for cuts from iron, but in his anger and frustration he could not remember it.

There was nothing to do but climb into the sledge and rush off to the next village for help.

"Is there anyone here who can heal the wounds of iron?" he shouted as he drove through the village. Only one old man answered yes. With his mighty word-spell, the old man stopped the bleeding, and called for his son to bind Väinämöinen's knee.

Limping back to his sledge, Väinä drove on south. He thought that perhaps the Maid was not a suitable wife for him after all.

Louhi was not very pleased when she learned how her daughter had amused herself with Väinämöinen.

"You should not have offered me for a Sampo!" answered the Maid. "You know I don't want to be married—and certainly not to an old man!"

"It was just a manner of speaking," said Louhi. "I meant I would not oppose the match. You could do worse, my girl!" Louhi went on, "You should treat Väinä with more respect. He's the greatest magician in the South, and he's promised to send us a master smith to forge a magic Sampo. How else would we get a Sampo?"

"I think Väinä will forget all about it once he is in his homeland," answered the Maid scornfully.

"No," said Louhi. "He will keep his promise to send the smith."

But Väinämöinen was not at all sure he *could* keep his promise. Suppose Ilmarinen did not want to go to the North Land? Thinking it was best to be prepared before he saw his friend, he went to the edge of a grain field near his home and began to sing a magic song. As he sang, a great pine tree with golden needles grew before him, reaching high into the sky. He sang a shining moon onto the very top, and the stars of the Great Bear onto the upper branches.

Well pleased with his work, he went off to the smithy where Ilmarinen the Sky Maker wielded his mighty hammer.

"Where have you been all this while?" asked the young smith.

"I've been to the North Land," said Väinä. "You should visit it, Seppo. It's a wonderful place!"

"Not from what I've heard," his friend retorted. "I've heard tales about the North Land. It's said the people there eat each other and drown heroes! It's not a place I'd want to visit!"

"Ah, but Seppo, the girls there!" Väinä said slyly. "You need a wife, and the Maid of the North is a charming, delightful girl. Beautiful dark hair and dark eyes—quite different from the fair-haired girls here."

"I'm not ready to marry," said Seppo, "and I'm not particularly interested in girls. So why should I go to that cold, bleak country?" He laid down his hammer. "What's behind all this, Väinä?"

"Old Louhi will give her daughter, the Maid of the North, to whoever makes her a magic Sampo," said Väinä.

"How does that concern you? I'm the only one who could make a magic Sampo," Ilmarinen said slowly. "What have you done? Promised Louhi I would make it?"

Väinämöinen turned red. "It's a mere trifle for a great smith like you. But truly, Seppo, it's a strange, marvelous country. Come see what I've brought back from the North—a pine tree with needles of gold, and the moon and the stars in its branches."

"I don't believe it! There's nothing in the North but snow and ice."

"Forget about the Sampo and the Maid. I can see you're not interested in marriage or in going to the North Land. But come with me and I'll show you one of the wonders of the North."

The smith followed Väinä to the edge of the field. There indeed stood the pine tree Väinä had described!

"You think it is only an illusion? Climb up into the pine tree and touch one of the stars," said Väinä complacently.

Now, Ilmarinen was the greatest master smith in Kalevala, but he was a simple, straightforward young man, easily beguiled. He began to climb the pine tree.

As soon as Seppo neared the upper branches, Väinämöinen began to sing up a storm. The wind rose, and lashed wildly through the branches.

Then, at Väinä's command, the wind bore Seppo Ilmarinen off through the air, high above the forests and lakes, to deposit him right inside old Louhi's front gate.

When Seppo looked around him, he knew he was in the North Land in spite of himself. His old friend Väinä had tricked him.

Old Louhi hurried out of the house to greet the stranger. "Where are you from, stranger? How did you get here? The watchdogs did not bark!"

"The way I came, a watchdog would be afraid to bark!" answered Seppo, still resentful.

Louhi looked puzzled. "Oh? Never mind, come in. You're welcome at our table."

The farm was much larger and more comfortable than Seppo had expected in the North Land, and the dinner set before him was not one he could complain about, either. When a tall, dark-haired girl with sparkling eyes and a merry smile came into the room, his interest was caught at once.

"Ah!" said the Maid. "I see we have another hero from the South."

"My daughter has many suitors," said Louhi hastily. "Tell me, young man, have you ever heard of Ilmarinen the great smith and master craftsman? We have been expecting him. He is to make me a magic Sampo."

"I am Ilmarinen the Master Smith, sometimes called Seppo by my friends," he answered.

"So you are Ilmarinen! Can you forge a magic Sampo for us?"

"It was I who hammered out the vault of the heavens," he answered simply.

"A Sampo should be an easy thing for a craftsman like you to make!" Noting the way he gazed at her daughter, Louhi added slyly, "In return, would you like this charming girl for a bride?" Ilmarinen thought old Väinä had not done him such an ill turn after all in sending him to the North Land. Väinä was right—the Maid was a delightful girl.

"I will make you the magic Sampo," said Seppo. "Where is your smithy?"

Louhi had to admit there was neither furnace nor forge—nor bellows, nor hammer and anvil. All these would have to be made first, before Ilmarinen could forge a magic Sampo. This was discouraging, but Seppo told himself cheerfully, "Heroes never despair!"

Louhi willingly supplied men to help Ilmarinen build the smithy and to work the bellows once the forge was completed. But even with the forge made, the work of making the Sampo went slowly.

At last, after many trials and errors, a splendid magic Sampo, with a top of many colors, was finished. When pressure was applied to a lever, the Sampo ground out flour meal from one side, salt from another, and coins from the third side. After it had ground out several barrels full of flour, salt, and coins, Louhi had it carried to the Copper Mountain and secured with locks. It was her most valuable treasure, and she didn't intend to have it stolen.

Ilmarinen, weary and black with soot, took a bath in the sauna. Then he presented himself to Louhi.

"Mistress Louhi, I have made the magic Sampo for you. May I have your daughter for my wife?"

Before Louhi could think of an evasive answer, the Maid of the North said, "Did you think I would leave the pine forests and sweet meadows of the North Land, where I can hear the cuckoos and the bluebirds sing in summer? Where I can roam at will to gather flowers and berries? Why should I go off to a strange land with a husband? No, thank you! I do not intend to marry so soon!"

Ilmarinen stared unhappily at the floor. So much for Louhi's fine offer! He had fallen in love with the Maid. Now he realized sadly that she would not leave the carefree life of her mother's farm to become a wife. He would have to return home without her.

Louhi bustled about to set a rich feast before

him. Then she gave him a boat with a copper paddle and called the north wind to blow him safely home. On the third day he was home in his own smithy.

He was building a fire in his cold furnace when old Väinä showed up.

"Well, Seppo? Did you make the magic Sampo for Mistress Louhi?"

"Yes, I forged it," said Ilmarinen with a sigh. "Much good it did me! The Maid of the North refused to have me for a husband."

"Never mind," said old Väinä, quite relieved at this news. "There are plenty of fair-haired girls here in Kalevala who will be glad to marry you."

"I'm not interested," muttered Ilmarinen.

Väinä went away feeling rather pleased. "So the Maid refused handsome young Seppo!" he said to himself. "I wonder if she still thinks of me? Perhaps she is sorry she teased the oldest, most powerful magician in Kalevala!" Still dazzled by the vision of the laughing Maid of the North seated on a rainbow, old Väinä decided he would not give up the idea of marrying her. She had asked for a boat made from the wood of her loom, he remembered. Very well, he would build a mighty boat, the most splendid boat ever made, and sail back to the North Country.

While Väinä was felling great oaks for his boat, another hero arrived at Louhi's farm. He was the vain dandy Kauko called Lemminkäinen, the Great Lover. Although he believed all the girls in Kalevala were charmed by him, he thought the girls of the South much too giddy. He had already gotten rid of one wife because she would not sit quietly at home as he demanded.

"I am Kauko Lemminkäinen, the great singer of songs, and I come from the Land of Heroes," he announced. "I know more magic songs and spells than anyone in the North Land."

"Indeed!" said Louhi. "And what is that to us?" She looked him over, not liking what she saw—a rude fellow, too full of his own importance.

"I've come to marry your daughter, the Maid of the North," he told her. "Where is she?"

"Marry the Maid? Not likely!" she scoffed. "Whatever put that idea into your head?"

"It's said in Kalevala that the Maid of the North refused old Väinä and young Seppo. And who can blame her? A charmer like that is the wife for Lemminkäinen!"

"You'd have to go out and capture the Great Elk of Hiisi the Evil One before I'd even consider such

18

a match!" This was Louhi's sharp way of saying no, for to capture the Elk of Hiisi the Evil One was an almost impossible task. Many heroes had tried it.

Lemminkäinen smiled in a superior way, put on his skis, and strapped a pack on his back. "I am a mighty hunter. There's not a four-footed creature in the land that can escape me," he boasted. And Hiisi the Evil One heard his boast.

The Maid of the North came outside with Louhi to watch Lemminkäinen disappear into the distance.

"I hope you don't fancy that one for a husband," said Louhi.

"Not at all!" said the Maid. "Why should I want to marry a noisy little rooster like that?"

Lemminkäinen chased the Great Elk of Hiisi day and night, uphill and downhill. He glided along with amazing speed until he chased the Great Elk to the far end of the North Country and came up at last beside the creature. He threw his lasso over its head, tamed the Elk with words, and dragged it back to Louhi's farm.

"Mistress, I've caught the Elk of Hiisi for you," said Lemminkäinen. "Now give me the Maid."

"Not so fast!" cried Louhi, thinking quickly of another way to get rid of him. "You must bridle and bring back the Wild Horse of Hiisi for me."

"That shouldn't be too difficult," said he. Strapping on his skis, off he went with a bridle of silver cleverly worked with gold. Again he traveled swiftly over the cold North Land day and night, until he came upon the Evil One's Wild Horse. The mighty stallion was a terrifying sight. His mane was a mass of fiery flames, and a cloud of smoke poured from his nostrils.

But Lemminkäinen put out the flames with powerful word-spells. Once the flames were gone, the stallion was tame. It was quite easy to put on the bridle of gold and silver and ride the horse back to Louhi.

When Louhi saw him ride into the farmyard on Hiisi's Wild Horse, she thought with irritation, "These heroes from Kalevala with their magic word-spells! But I won't have this arrogant fellow wooing the Maid."

"Well, Mistress!" cried Lemminkäinen triumphantly. "Here's the Horse of Hiisi. Now the Maid—"

"I can see that you're a proper hero!" said Louhi. She went on craftily, "I said I'd consider your offer, and I will. There's one last thing you must do—you must shoot the White Swan of Tuonela* with a single arrow."

* In Finnish mythology, Tuonela is the realm of the dead.

This was the most dangerous of the tasks she had set, for the White Swan lived on the river of Tuoni, the Lord of the Dead. Many heroes had sought the White Swan and never returned.

Taking his bow and quiver of arrows, Lemminkäinen set off confidently for the dark lands of Tuonela. When he at last found the river, running black through the dark rocks and caverns in the Land of the Dead, he stood uncertainly on the bank. He peered through the gloom, waiting for a sight of the White Swan.

But Hiisi the Evil One now took his revenge. From the dark, tumbled rocks on the bank, Hiisi loosed a poisonous serpent who sank his fangs into Lemminkäinen's heart. The young hunter crumpled to the ground, dead.

And that would have been the end of Lemminkäinen, had not his mother possessed considerable magical power of her own. Far away in Kalevala, she knew at once that evil had befallen her son. Journeying to the far North and on into the dreadful lands of Tuoni, she found her son's body where it had fallen.

Her word charms had no effect. Her son lay still and cold. Summoning a bee, she bade her fly to the fields of Ukko, the Creator of Life, and bring back honey. The bee flew off at once and returned with the precious drops of life. These she rubbed all over her son's body.

"Wake from this sleep of evil dreams," she sang. "Rise, my son, and leave this wicked place."

Lemminkäinen stretched and woke. "I have slept a long time."

"You would have slept forever if it hadn't been for me," said his mother.

He looked into the dark gloom around them. "Where am I?"

"You're in Tuonela, and the faster we leave here, the better," said his mother briskly.

"But I must shoot the White Swan of Tuonela if I'm to win the Maid of the North," he cried.

His mother looked at him with exasperation. "You don't realize the narrow escape you've had! Let the Swan alone and forget the Maid of the North. She's not for you. Come along back to Kalevala with me and choose a girl of your own kind."

For once, Lemminkäinen took his mother's advice. He returned to the South, and Louhi and the Maid were well pleased to be rid of him.

By this time, old Väinä had finished his boat. It was without doubt the finest, strongest boat in Kalevala. He had painted it red and decorated the prow and sides with gold. Early one morning, he brought provisions aboard and hoisted a red and blue sail.

Early as it was, Annikki, Ilmarinen's sister, was up even earlier, washing clothes at the edge of the shore.

"Where are you going, Väinä?" she called.

"Salmon fishing. The salmon trout are spawning."

"Don't tell me a silly lie," said Annikki. "You have no nets or tackle. And besides, it's not the season."

"I'm going after wild geese," said Väinä impatiently.

"Another lie!" she laughed. "You have no bow or hunting dogs. Tell me honestly where you are going, Väinä."

"Well," said the old magician, "I did lie a little. Actually I'm going off to the cold and misty North Land."

When Annikki heard this, she dropped her washing and ran as fast as she could to the smithy.

"Seppo!" she called to her brother.

He laid down his hammer. "What is it?"

"I have interesting news for you. And I think I deserve earrings and a ring for bringing it to you!"

"I'll make you the trinkets if the news is important," said Seppo.

"Are you still thinking of that girl up in the North Land?" Of course, Annikki knew very well that Seppo was still brooding over the tall, dark-haired Maid. "Do you still want to marry her?"

Seppo stared at her. "And if I do?"

"Well, you've done nothing about it! While you are here working your head off at the forge, crafty old Väinä has just set sail for the North Land."

It took Ilmarinen only a few moments to realize what this meant. "I'm going on a journey. Get the bathhouse ready for me, Annikki. I'll need a steam bath to wash off this soot. Kindle a fire of chips, get the stones hot, and bring plenty of soap. While you're doing that, I'll gladly make you the ring and earrings!"

Annikki hurried to gather firewood for the sauna. When at last she came to tell her brother the bathhouse was ready, he had made her not only a ring and earrings, but a slender silver girdle as well.

Ilmarinen rubbed and scrubbed and steamed himself until his skin and hair were shining. He dressed carefully in a fine linen shirt, trousers, and stockings his mother had woven. He pulled on smooth leather boots. Then he put on a blue coat lined with red, and over that a furred, heavy wool cape. His sister handed him warm gloves, and his mother gave him a handsome fur hat his father had worn as a bridegroom. Dressed at last, the tall, powerful Ilmarinen looked very splendid indeed.

While the horse was being harnessed to the sledge and his gear packed, Ilmarinen had a servant fetch six golden cuckoos to sit on the frame and seven singing bluebirds to perch on the reins. Thick furs were brought for him to sit on, and to cover him against the northern cold.

Cracking his whip, he drove off along the shore at a steady pace until, on the third day, he overtook his old friend Väinämöinen, sailing out on the waters.

"Väinä!" he called. "Let's make a friendly agreement so there'll be no hard feelings. Let us agree the Maid shall choose freely and fairly between us."

"I agree to that," answered Väinä. He was sure the Maid would choose himself, the wise, old magician, the greatest singer among the heroes. Nonetheless, he got out the oars and rowed to help speed the boat along.

Not long after this, the watchdogs at Louhi's farm began to bark furiously. Louhi sent out the serving maid to see who approached.

"Strangers are coming," she reported when she returned to the house. "Someone in a sledge and another rowing a red boat."

Louhi had the serving maid put a new log on the fire. "If the log sweats blood, the strangers bring trouble," said Louhi. "If it sweats water, they come in peace."

They all watched the log intently. But it sweated neither blood nor water. The new log oozed honey. Louhi tasted a drop to be sure. "This means the strangers are noble suitors!" she exclaimed.

She hurried out to the gates to see for herself. Now the red boat with the elegant gold swirls on the prow was pulling to the shore. Handling the oars was the gray-haired, gray-bearded hero, Väinämöinen. The sledge drew near, gay with singing birds perched on the reins. She saw with misgiving that the splendidly dressed driver was Ilmarinen, the smith who had forged her magic Sampo.

"Those two heroes from the South are here again," said old Louhi as she came back into the house. "Väinämöinen brings great treasure in his boat, I'll wager. The young Seppo brings nothing but his fine clothes and singing birds!"

"Singing birds?" The Maid began to smile. "Are they cuckoos and bluebirds?" She ran to the door to look for Seppo's sledge.

Louhi called her back impatiently. "It's time you made up your mind about marriage. You'll have to choose between them. I advise you to draw a cup of mead and offer it to the man of your choice." The Maid was silent.

"I leave it to you to choose," her mother went on briskly, "but if you have an ounce of sense, you'll take my advice and choose old Väinä. He's the wisest and most powerful of all the heroes—and besides, he's loaded with treasure."

"I'm not interested in money or treasure, nor in the power of an old man. When I marry, it will be a strong young man," said the Maid stubbornly. "Ilmarinen is a master craftsman. He may not be as wise or as powerful with word-spells as old Väinä— but he did make the magic Sampo!"

"Don't be foolish," said old Louhi sharply, for she had made up her mind she would like to have the great magician Väinämöinen for her son-in-law. "If you marry a smith, he'll be covered with sweat and soot most of the time. Think of all that washing—you'll spend every day scrubbing the soot from his clothes!"

"I don't care about that," said the Maid.

Just then, Väinä entered the house. "Fair Maid of the North," he said politely, "will you marry me? Remember, you asked me once to make a boat from your loom? I did have a little trouble with that, but now I have made a magnificent boat, strong enough to sail the seas and weather every tempest."

"I don't care for sailors," said the Maid coolly. "Marry a man who thinks so much of boats he's always sailing off somewhere for another adventure? No, Väinä, I will not be your wife."

Before Väinä could plead his case, Ilmarinen came in. When he pulled off his hat, the firelight gleamed brightly on his thick golden hair. It was over a year since Seppo had lived with them to make the magic Sampo. He now seemed even more attractive than the Maid remembered.

"Did you really bring singing birds from Kalevala on your sledge, Seppo?" asked the Maid.

"Six cuckoos and seven bluebirds," he answered shyly.

The Maid of the North brought the large cup of mead to Ilmarinen and put it into his hands.

But Seppo only held it before him carefully. "I will not drink the mead until I have your answer. For many, many months I have thought of you and longed for you. If you do not accept me this time, I will not return again."

The Maid gave him a radiant smile. Before she could speak, Louhi cut in quickly.

"I see she has made her choice. That's all very well, but there's something you must do for me first. Not far away there is a Field of Vipers that must be plowed."

"Yes, yes . . . of course," stammered Ilmarinen.

"Hiisi the Evil One dumped them there, and it's a great nuisance to me—" began Louhi. Then she saw that old Väinämöinen had left quietly to return to his boat. She hurried after him to be sure he was well stocked with provisions.

When the Maid and Seppo were alone, he turned to her with a puzzled frown. "I don't think your mother wants you to marry me. A Field of Vipers! Does she want me killed so you will marry Väinä?"

"I would never marry Väinä," she assured him. "But this task is not as difficult as it sounds, my dear. I can tell you how to do it. Forge for yourself a coat of mail, iron boots, and iron gloves, so the vipers cannot touch you. Then forge a plow of gold and silver to make them leave. With these things you will plow the field safely."

Ilmarinen went off to the forge where he had once made the magic Sampo. He followed the Maid's instructions, then set off, clad in the iron garments.

The Field of Vipers, filled with small, twisting serpents, was a horrible place to see. Seppo hesitated but a moment before setting the gold and silver plow into the field. Chanting the spell against serpents, he strode into the mass of writhing snakes. Their fangs snapped, but could not harm him through his metal garments. In a very short time they all slipped away from the field and disappeared. When the field was plowed in clean, even strips, he returned to the farmhouse.

"I have plowed the field, Mistress," he told Louhi. "Now may I marry your daughter?"

"Not yet," said crafty Louhi. "You must capture the Great Bear and the Great Wolf that live in the forest of Tuoni, the Lord of the Dead. Bring them to me—and then we'll see." Louhi knew very well that many heroes had tried to capture these beasts without success.

Seppo went off to find the Maid. "My love, I think your mother wishes me harm!" he exclaimed. "She wants me to capture the Great Bear and the

Great Wolf from the Land of the Dead! I'll be torn to pieces!"

"Perhaps my mother only wants to be sure I marry a great hero," said the Maid thoughtfully. "Do not worry, Seppo. I know how it can be done. Listen carefully. Sit on a rock under the spray of a waterfall and forge two iron muzzles. With these the Great Bear and the Great Wolf of Tuoni can be easily captured.

Ilmarinen followed the Maid's advice. When he had forged the huge muzzles of hard iron and attached chains to them, he set out for the forest of Tuoni. He crept cautiously through the forest until he came upon the Great Bear. Leaping from behind, he muzzled the beast and left him chained to a tree. He captured the Wolf in the same way. Then, using all his strength, he dragged the two animals back to Louhi's farm.

"Here they are," he panted. "Much good may they do you!"

Louhi nodded in approval. "It seems you're a proper hero after all. Now there's just one more task before I arrange the wedding feast. Bring me the Great Pike that swims in Tuoni's river—without using a net or a line." Plenty of heroes have tried *that*, she thought, and not returned.

Ilmarinen left her and again sought out the Maid

to tell her of the task that had been laid on him. "This is too much!" he cried angrily. "Catch that monstrous Pike with my bare hands? He would chew me up in a moment!"

"My darling, only you can do it," she said proudly. "I will tell you how. Forge a huge bird of fire and flame, with claws of iron. The bird will catch the Pike for you, and you will not be harmed."

Once more, Ilmarinen set to work in the forge. When he had made the huge metal bird of fire and flame, he climbed on its back and was borne swiftly to the shores of the river of Tuoni. There they waited until the Great Pike rose to the surface. And what a monster he proved to be! His body was as long as seven boats, and his sharp teeth filled a mouth as long as two rake handles.

The iron bird leaped onto the Pike at once, seizing it in its claws. A long and furious battle raged between them, for the Pike had great power in its jaws and tried to drag the bird of iron under the water. At last the Great Pike was killed, and the huge bird flew up to the top of a pine tree with the fish. There he ripped it apart with its claws and began to eat it.

With a roar of rage, Seppo ordered the bird to stop. "I must bring that Pike to Louhi!" he shouted. "Drop it at once!"

The great bird tossed down the head. Then, with a sweep of its huge wings, it flew off out of sight with the remainder of the Pike in its beak.

Ilmarinen dragged the long head of the Pike back to Louhi's farm.

"Here's the head of your Great Pike!" he growled. "You can make a long bench from the bones if you wish!"

"I asked for the Great Pike itself, not the head," Louhi began. But when she saw the expression on Seppo's face, she decided to drop the matter.

"You can marry the Maid," she said hastily, "and sorry I'll be to lose her."

And so it was settled at last. While Seppo hurried back to his home with the news, Louhi began the preparations for the wedding feast.

An enormous hall was built to feed and house the guests. The Great Ox of Carelia was slaughtered to provide hundreds of barrels of meat and hundreds of barrels of sausages. Hundreds of barrels of ale and hundreds of barrels of mead were brewed. More than half of all the fish in the rivers and lakes were caught. There seemed no end to the mountains of food and drink.

Never had the North Land seen such a feast! All the people of the North Land and all the people of Kalevala were invited to the wedding, and most of them came. The people flocked to Louhi's farm from all directions—by sledge, by boat, by skis. And Seppo, at the head of a small army of joyful kinfolk, arrived on the appointed day.

The feasting and singing and merrymaking went on for seven days and seven nights. Then at last it was time for the Maid of the North to take off her richly embroidered wedding garments and prepare for the journey south to Kalevala.

Seppo's sledge was ready, gay with singing birds on the reins. The bridal couple were settled under fur robes. The whip cracked and they moved off amid the cheers and good wishes of the guests.

And that is the story of how the Maid of the North left her beloved North Country to live with the Master Smith Ilmarinen in Kalevala.

While many retellings and translations of this story exist today, this version of "The Maid of the North" was drawn from the Kalevala *(1907) translated by* **WILLIAM FORSELL KIRBY**. *The* Kalevala *is a Finnish national saga that explores traditional creation stories, magic and the supernatural, and the epic adventures of heroes in the North Lands.*

There once was a young woman who was alone in the world except for her child. She had only a cow, a few chickens, and a small garden to get by on. To earn a little money she would go out to work in the fields at haying and harvest time.

One day she laid the baby on a rough piece of cloth in the shade of an old hawthorn tree, picked up a scythe, and took her place with the hay mowers.

The lass had mowed several lengths of the field when she heard the baby wailing with hunger. She hurried to the hawthorn tree, thinking that the wailing did not sound at all like her sweet-tempered baby.

When she got there, she saw that it was not her plump, dark-haired child that lay in the shade—it was a thin, scrawny baby with wisps of fair hair.

She ran up and down the side of the field, searching for her own child, but there was no sign of him. She called to the other mowers. No one had seen her baby, nor had they seen anyone come to the hawthorn tree.

She went back to the wailing baby, her heart breaking with grief. Then, because she was a kind-hearted lass, she took pity on the thin, pale child. She could not bear to see him so hungry, so she nursed him.

With a heavy heart she returned to the mowing, for she needed the money. But when the day was over, she felt she could not abandon the sickly child in the field all night. She carried the small bundle home with her.

That evening and all the next day, she went up and down the lanes of the village, asking everyone she met if they had seen her dark-haired, rosy-cheeked baby.

No one had seen him. "The fairy folk have taken your child and left a sickly one of their own in his place," she was told. "You must get rid of the changeling if you want your own back." But the advice they gave on how to get rid of the changeling was so cruel that she could not follow it.

She made up her mind to get her own child back from the fairies, though how she was to do it she did not know. Nonetheless, as the weeks passed, she fed and cared for the strange, pale child as best she could. He no longer looked quite so frail and thin. His wisps of hair grew into thick red-gold curls; he would soon be as plump and healthy as her own child.

"Your mother should see you now," thought the lass one day. "You're so healthy and handsome she wouldn't know you!"

The summer had gone before the lass heard of an old woman who was said to know the ways of the fairy folk. Although the woman lived alone out on the moors, some distance away, the lass trudged off at once to consult her.

After she had told the old woman of her stolen child, she said, "Do you know where the fairy folk dwell? I'm determined to get my own child back."

"You're a brave lass," said the old woman. "But do you know the danger in it?"

"That doesn't matter," answered the lass.

"They can lame or blind those who annoy them—or do worse mischief," warned the old woman. "They could keep you prisoner under the fairy hill forever."

"I wouldn't like that, but if I were with my own child again—"

"But, lass, if you go to their fairy hill, you'd be putting yourself in their power!" When the lass did not answer, the woman sighed, "Well, if you won't be warned, I'll tell you what I can."

"That is what I came for," said the lass.

"The fairy folk live under that big hill out yonder on the moors," said the woman. "They don't come out very often, and when they do, there are few that can see them."

"Have you seen them?" asked the girl directly.

"Sometimes," the woman admitted. "I did them a favor long ago, and they've been good neighbors to me."

"I want to see the Queen," said the girl firmly. "She will know who took my baby."

"The Queen and all the folk come out of the hill on Halloween to ride abroad. That I do know. But it will do you no good. She'll fly into a rage if you demand your child back."

"I can try," said the girl.

"Don't expect the Queen to take pity on your

grief. Fairy folk have no hearts, no hearts at all. 'Tis the way they are made."

"I'll not ask for pity," said the lass. "All I'll ask is a fair exchange."

"It's not a thing I'd dare to do," said the old woman.

The lass walked out to the fairy hill at once, for she thought she might find a way in. She walked all around it, poking at rocks, pulling at bushes, but she could see no opening at all. At last she gave up and came away. She made up her mind to come back on Halloween.

The weeks passed slowly. Finally the nuts ripened and fell, and the leaves turned yellow and red and drifted from the trees.

On Halloween the lass milked the cow, fed the baby, and, wrapping him against the chill, started off for the fairy hill.

The night was dark, with heavy clouds scudding across the moon. It was a long way out to the fairy hill on the moors, and the baby grew heavy in her arms. She paused to rest now and then, but not for long. When she reached the moors, it was so dark she couldn't see the hill. Twice she turned the wrong way.

At last she reached the hill and sank wearily to the ground. She had no way of knowing if she was too early or too late—nor even which part of the hill would open to send the fairy folk forth.

She waited in the silence and the dark. After a little while her head nodded in weariness, and she dozed.

It was near midnight when she was jerked awake by the sound of silvery bells. Flowing out of the hill, some distance from where she sat, was a troop of fairy folk. The Queen rode before them on a white steed. In the glow of their own eerie fairy light, she could see that the Queen was splendidly dressed in green and gold, her gleaming red-gold hair flying behind her.

The lass jumped to her feet, but the fairy folk came out of the hill with the rush of a strong wind and were off in a flurry of jingling bells. The eerie fairy glow died away, and she was left standing on the empty moor in the moonlight.

For a few moments she was overcome with

despair. Then she said to herself with a sigh, "I never expected it would be easy!"

She stood for a moment, fixing in her mind by means of rocks and bushes just where the fairy hill had opened. "I'll stand right in their path next time," she thought.

She went back to where the changeling lay asleep and carried him all the long way home. It was near dawn when she opened the door to her small cottage, and there was a day's work ahead of her.

The winter passed, cold with sleet and icy rain. The fair-haired changeling grew sturdier, but he was a silent child with a faraway look in his eyes. One spring day the lass met the old woman at market.

"I see you still have the changeling," said the old woman.

"Yes," said the lass. "My eyes closed for weariness on Halloween, but I shall try again. Will the fairy folk come out on May Eve?"

"They should," said the old woman. Then she added kindly, "Come early to my cottage and rest yourself before you set out."

"Thank you," said the lass. "I'll do that."

On May Eve she arrived at the old woman's cottage early. The changeling was now a plump, handsome child, although his skin still had the whiteness of fairy kind.

As soon as the sun set, the lass and the child went off to the fairy hill. She put the child to sleep beside her and settled down for a long wait.

This time, when the hill opened with the jingling of silver bells on bridles, the lass was ready. The Queen rode out, splendidly radiant, at the head of the fairy folk.

The lass had placed herself in their path. Now she ran forward and caught the bridle of the Queen's steed. The Queen raised her staff as if to strike.

"Who dares to halt the Queen?" she cried in cold anger.

But before the Queen could blind or cripple her, the lass cried out, "If you please, ma'am, I have brought you a gift."

The whole company of folk halted behind the Queen were still.

"A gift? What manner of talk is this?" asked the Queen irritably, but her interest was caught.

At this moment the child woke, cried aloud, and stood up.

"Who is that child? Why do you bring him here?"

The lass went to the child and held him firmly at her side. "He's a handsome child, isn't he?"

"Is this the gift?" asked the Queen coolly, but her eyes stared at the child.

"In a manner of speaking," said the lass, just as

coolly. "He was left in a hayfield last summer—a thin, sickly thing. Do you remember?"

The Queen said nothing.

"I took him home with me, fed him, cared for him, brought him to health. I was pleased to do a favor for one of your women. Do you know his mother?"

"I *am* his mother," said the Queen curtly.

"I thought he'd be of royal stock—he's that handsome and clever a child!" said the lass, thinking a bit of flattery would do no harm.

"So you've brought him back to the fairy folk!" said the Queen in surprise. "Didn't you want to keep him?"

"He's of fairy stock; I don't think he'll thrive for long in the outside world," said the lass. "And that seems a pity."

"Hand him up to me," said the Queen. "I want to see if this is really my child."

"No," said the lass. "I've done you a favor, and now I ask one in return. I want my own son back."

The Queen frowned. "I could seize the child."

"You could," admitted the lass, and her heart shook within her. "But I did you a favor, nursed your child, shared the little food I had with him. It's said that fairy folk repay favors honestly. All I ask is a fair exchange. I want my own child back."

The Queen laughed. "You have cool courage,

girl. Don't you know I could seize both of you and keep you in our hill?"

"I know that," said the lass steadily. "But I was thinking you'd want to repay the favor. He's a fine, handsome prince for your court."

Abruptly the Queen called to the folk behind her, "Bring the dark-haired child." Then, to the lass, "Now let me have this one."

"No," said the lass. "Not until I have my own in my arms."

"A stubborn lass!" commented the Queen. "You have no fear at all; I admire that. Well, here he is."

When the lass had her own child on the grass beside her, she handed the fair-haired boy up to the Queen.

The Queen held the child before her on the saddle. She said coolly, "He *is* a healthy, handsome child. You took care of him well." Then, looking down at the lass holding her own child tightly in her arms, she added, "Go in peace. The favor and goodwill of the fairy folk will stay with your child all his life."

With a rush of wind and a jingle of bells, they were away. The eerie fairy glow was gone. The lass was alone on the dark, empty moor.

Carrying her own child, she walked with a light heart to the old woman's cottage.

As the Queen had promised, good fortune and prosperity came to the lass and her child and stayed with them ever after.

Many tales in rural Irish folklore include stories of "changelings," children switched at birth by fairies. Often these fairies were depicted as being willful and capricious, but ultimately fair and just to those who proved to be deserving. This story was largely rewritten, but mainly developed from an incident in **LADY WILDE***'s* Ancient Legends of Ireland *(1887).*

Long ago in China, a young girl lived in a small village at the foot of Horse Ear Mountain. Her name was Sea Girl and she lived with her father, a hard-working farmer.

No rain had fallen for many months; the crops hung limp and brown, dying for want of water. It seemed there could be no harvest, and food was already scarce. So each day Sea Girl went up on Horse Ear Mountain and cut bamboo to make brooms to sell.

One day when Sea Girl had climbed higher on the mountain than ever before in her search for bamboo, she saw a large blue lake gleaming in the sun. The water of the lake was clear and still. Not a single fallen leaf marred its surface, for whenever a leaf fell from the trees surrounding the lake, a large wild goose flew down and carried it away. This was the Wild Goose Lake Sea Girl had heard the elders speak of in the village tales.

Sea Girl carried her bamboo home, thinking of the clear blue water of the lake and how badly the people needed water for their crops.

The next day she took her ax to cut bamboo and again climbed high in the mountain. She hoped she could make an outlet from Wild Goose Lake. The village harvest would be saved if the lake water trickled down the mountain in a gentle stream to the farms below.

She began to walk around the lake, following the narrow, sandy shore. But the lake was surrounded by jagged rocks, high cliffs, and dense forest. There seemed to be no place to make an outlet for a stream. Later in the day, she came upon a thick stone gate. Her ax was of no help, and although she used all her strength, the gate could not be moved.

Wearily she dropped her pile of bamboo cuttings and sat down next to the gate. All was still, and the lake was a mirror reflecting the dark green pines. A wild goose swooped high in the sky, then glided down to stand on the ground nearby.

"Sea Girl," said the Wild Goose, "you will need the Golden Key to open the gate."

Before she could ask where she could find the Golden Key, the wild goose spread her wings and soared away over the lake. Sea Girl noticed a small keyhole in the stone gate, but there was no key.

Sea Girl walked on along the shore of the lake, searching for the Golden Key. She came to a forest of cypress trees, and sitting on a cypress branch was a brilliant parrot of scarlet and green.

"Parrot," she called, "do you know where I can find the Golden Key that will open the stone gate?"

The parrot answered, "You must first find the third daughter of the Dragon King, for the Dragon King guards the Golden Key to Wild Goose Lake." With a quick whirring of wings the parrot flew off into the forest.

Sea Girl walked on, searching for the Dragon King's third daughter. In a pine grove close to the lake, she saw a peacock sitting on a low branch.

"Peacock, peacock," she called, "where can I find the Dragon King's third daughter?"

"The Dragon King's third daughter loves songs. If you sing the songs your village people sing, she will come forth from the lake." The peacock dropped a feather at her feet and flew away.

Sea Girl picked up the feather and began to sing. Her voice was clear, and as fresh as a lark's song. At first she sang about the snowflakes drifting on the mountains, but the Dragon King's third daughter did not appear. She sang of green reeds bending in the wind. Still the third daughter did not come; the lake lay clear and still. Then Sea Girl sang of pale blossoming flowers on the hills.

Near the shore the water broke into a glittering spray, and the third daughter came up out of the lake to stand before Sea Girl.

"Deep in the lake I heard your songs," she said. "They are so strange and beautiful that I could not resist them. My father does not allow us to meet humans, but I have come to you secretly. I, too, love songs, and your songs are finer than mine."

Sea Girl asked, "Are you the third daughter of the Dragon King?"

"Yes, I am Third Daughter. My father and his people guard Wild Goose Lake. Who are you? Why do you sing your songs here?"

"I am Sea Girl. I live in a village at the foot of Horse Ear Mountain, and I have come all this long way to find the Golden Key which opens the stone gate of the lake. The people in my village are hungry and need water to save their harvest."

Third Daughter hesitated, then she said, "I would like to help you. The Golden Key is kept in my father's treasure room, deep in a rock cave. Outside on the cliff a huge eagle guards it, and he would tear to pieces anyone who tried to enter." She pointed to a rock cliff a little distance off. On the cliff perched an eagle nodding in the sun.

Sea Girl asked, "Would your father give us the Golden Key?"

"He will not help humans," sighed Third Daughter. "That is why he had the stone gate made to keep in the lake water. You must wait until my father leaves his palace and goes off. Then perhaps we can lure the eagle away from the treasure room."

So Sea Girl made a bed of soft pine branches under the trees and Third Daughter brought her fresh fish to eat.

A few days later she said to Sea Girl, "My father has left his palace. Now is the time to search for the key, but I don't know how you will slip past the eagle."

"We will sing to him," said Sea Girl.

The two girls lightly and quietly moved closer

to where the eagle perched high on the rock cliff. Third Daughter pointed out the entrance to the cave below. Tall ferns and reeds hid the girls from sight, and they began to sing. Each took turns singing the loveliest and most enchanting songs they knew.

At first the eagle just peered around curiously. Then, drawn by the strange haunting sounds, he flew down from the cliff in search of the source. Third Daughter crept quietly farther and farther away, and the eagle followed the enchanting sound of her voice.

Sea Girl slipped into the treasure cave to search for the Golden Key. At first her eyes were dazzled, for the room was filled on all sides with gold, silver, and sparkling jewels. But Sea Girl did not touch the treasure. She searched only for the Golden Key.

Just as she was about to give up in despair, she saw a small, plain wooden box sitting on a shelf in the corner. Quickly she opened it and peered in. There lay the gleaming Golden Key!

Sea Girl took the key and returned to where Third Daughter waited. When the delicate soaring melody of song ceased, the eagle shook himself, spread his wings, and sailed back to his cliff.

Sea Girl and Third Daughter hastened back to

the stone gate. The Golden Key fitted perfectly into the keyhole, and the gate swung open. At once the water rushed out in a leaping cascade, down the mountainside to the village. In a very short time, all the canals and ditches of the farms were full and overflowing with water.

Third Daughter saw that the village would soon be flooded and she called out, "Sea Girl, Sea Girl, there is too much water. The crops will be washed away and lost!"

Sea Girl quickly threw in the piles of bamboo she had left earlier at the stone gate. But that slowed the water only a little. Then the two girls rolled boulders and large rocks into the stream until the water slowed down to a small, bubbling brook. Now they knew the village would always have a steady supply of water.

When the Dragon King returned and found the Golden Key was gone, he was very angry. He banished Third Daughter from the palace. But Third Daughter went to live very happily with Sea Girl, and they sang their songs together as they worked.

So beautiful were their songs that each year ever after, on the twenty-second day of the seventh moon, all the women of the surrounding villages came together to sing songs and celebrate the heroic deed of Sea Girl.

This version was adapted by the editor from a tale in Folktales of China *(1965), edited by* **WOLFRAM EBERHARD**. *The story comes from a minority group living in southwest China, the Yi tribes of Yunnan. However, the Dragon King is frequently found in Chinese tales, and the importance given to folk singing is typical of many groups in southern and western China.*

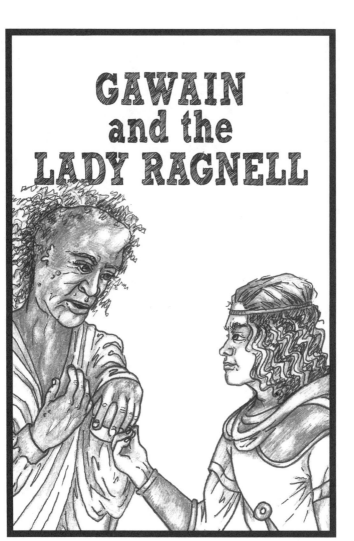

GAWAIN
and the
LADY RAGNELL

Long ago, in the days of King Arthur, the finest knight in all of Britain was the king's nephew Gawain. He was, by reputation, the bravest in battle, the wisest, the most courteous, the most compassionate, and the most loyal to his king.

One day in late summer, Gawain was with Arthur and the knights of the court at Carlisle in the North. The king returned from the day's hunting looking so pale and shaken that Gawain followed him at once to his chamber.

"What has happened, my lord?" asked Gawain with concern.

Arthur sat down heavily. "I had a very strange encounter in Inglewood Forest . . . I hardly know what to make of it." And he related to Gawain what had occurred.

"Today I hunted a great white stag," said Arthur.

"The stag at last escaped me, and I was alone, some distance from my men. Suddenly a tall, powerful man appeared before me with sword upraised."

"And you were unarmed!"

"Yes. I had only my bow and a dagger in my belt. He threatened to kill me," Arthur went on. "And he swung his sword as though he meant to cut me down on the spot! Then he laughed horribly and said he would give me one chance to save my life."

"Who was this man?" cried Gawain. "Why should he want to kill you?"

"He said his name was Sir Gromer, and he sought revenge for the loss of his northern lands."

"A chieftain from the North!" exclaimed Gawain. "But what is this one chance he spoke of?"

"I gave him my word I would meet him one year from today, unarmed, at the same spot, with the answer to a question!" said Arthur.

Gawain started to laugh, but stopped at once when he saw Arthur's face. "A question! Is it a riddle? And one year to find the answer? That should not be hard!"

"If I can bring him the true answer to the question 'What is it that women most desire, above all else?' my life will be spared." Arthur scowled. "He is sure I will fail. It must be a foolish riddle that no one can answer."

"My lord, we have one year to search the kingdom for answers," said Gawain confidently. "I will help you. Surely one of the answers will be the right one."

"No doubt you are right—someone will know the answer." Arthur looked more cheerful. "The man is mad, but a chieftain will keep his word."

For the next twelve months, Arthur and Gawain asked the question from one corner of the kingdom to the other. Then at last the appointed day drew near. Although they had many answers, Arthur was worried.

"With so many answers to choose from, how do we know which is the right one?" he asked in despair. "Not one of them has the ring of truth."

A few days before he was to meet Sir Gromer, Arthur rode out alone through the golden gorse and purple heather. The track led upward toward a grove of great oaks. Arthur, deep in thought, did not look up until he reached the edge of the oak wood. When he raised his head, he pulled up suddenly in astonishment.

Before him was a grotesque woman. She was almost as wide as she was high, her skin was mottled green, and spikes of weedlike hair covered her head. Her face seemed more animal than human.

The woman's eyes met Arthur's fearlessly. "You

are Arthur the king," she said in a harsh, croaking voice. "In two days time you must meet Sir Gromer with the answer to a question."

Arthur turned cold with fear. He stammered, "Yes . . . yes . . . that is true. Who are you? How did you know of this?"

"I am the Lady Ragnell. Sir Gromer is my step-brother. You haven't found the true answer, have you?"

"I have many answers," Arthur replied curtly. "I do not see how my business concerns you." He gathered up the reins, eager to be gone.

"You do not have the right answer." Her certainty filled him with a sense of doom. The harsh voice went on, "But I know the answer to Sir Gromer's question."

Arthur turned back in hope and disbelief. "You do? Tell me the true answer to his question, and I will give you a large bag of gold."

"I have no use for gold," she said coldly.

"Nonsense, my good woman. With gold you can buy anything you want!" He hesitated a moment, for the huge, grotesque face with the cool, steady eyes unnerved him. He went on hurriedly, "What is it you want? Jewelry? Land? Whatever you want I will pay you—that is, if you truly have the right answer."

"I know the answer. I promise you that!" She paused. "What I demand in return is that the knight Gawain become my husband."

There was a moment of shocked silence. Then Arthur cried, "Impossible! You ask the impossible, woman!"

She shrugged and turned to leave.

"Wait, wait a moment!" Rage and panic overwhelmed him, but he tried to speak reasonably.

"I offer you gold, land, jewels. I cannot give you my nephew. He is his own man. He is not mine to give!"

"I did not ask you to *give* me the knight Gawain," she rebuked him. "If Gawain himself agrees to marry me, I will give you the answer. Those are my terms."

"Impossible!" he sputtered. "I could not bring him such a proposal."

"If you should change your mind, I will be here tomorrow," said she, and disappeared into the oak woods.

Shaken from the weird encounter, Arthur rode homeward at a slow pace.

"Save my own life at Gawain's expense? Never!" he thought. "Loathsome woman! I could not even speak of it to Gawain."

But the afternoon air was soft and sweet with

birdsong, and the fateful meeting with Sir Gromer weighed on him heavily. He was torn by the terrible choice facing him.

Gawain rode out from the castle to meet the king. Seeing Arthur's pale, strained face, he exclaimed, "My lord! Are you ill? What has happened?"

"Nothing . . . nothing at all." But he could not keep silent long. "The colossal impudence of the woman! A monster, that's what she is! That creature, daring to give me terms!"

"Calm yourself, Uncle," Gawain said patiently. "What woman? Terms for what?"

Arthur sighed. "She knows the answer to the question. I didn't intend to tell you."

"Why not? Surely that's good news! What is the answer?"

"She will not tell me until her terms are met," said the king heavily. "But I assure you, I refuse to consider her proposal!"

Gawain smiled. "You talk in riddles yourself, Uncle. Who is this woman who claims to know the answer? What is her proposal?"

Seeing Gawain's smiling, expectant face, Arthur at first could not speak. Then, with his eyes averted, the king told Gawain the whole story, leaving out no detail.

"The Lady Ragnell is Sir Gromer's stepsister? Yes, I think she would know the right answer,"

Gawain said thoughtfully. "How fortunate that I will be able to save your life!"

"No! I will not let you sacrifice yourself!" Arthur cried.

"It is my choice and my decision," Gawain answered. "I will return with you tomorrow and agree to the marriage—on condition that the answer she supplies is the right one to save your life."

Early the following day, Gawain rode out with Arthur. But not even meeting the loathsome lady face-to-face could shake his resolve. Her proposal was accepted.

Gawain bowed courteously. "If on the morrow your answer saves the king's life, we will be wed."

On the fateful morning, Gawain watched the king stow a parchment in his saddlebag. "I'll try all these answers first," said Arthur.

They rode together for the first part of the journey. Then Arthur, unarmed as agreed, rode on alone to Inglewood to meet Sir Gromer.

The tall, powerful chieftain was waiting, his broadsword glinting in the sun.

Arthur read off one answer, then another, and another. Sir Gromer shook his head in satisfaction.

"No, you have not the right answer!" he said, raising his sword high. "You've failed, and now—"

"Wait!" Arthur cried. "I have one more answer.

What a woman desires above all else is the power of sovereignty—the right to exercise her own will."

With a loud oath the man dropped his sword. "You did not find that answer by yourself!" he shouted. "My cursed stepsister, Ragnell, gave it to you. Bold, interfering hussy! I'll run her through with my sword . . . I'll lop off her head . . ." Turning, he plunged into the forest, a string of horrible curses echoing behind him.

Arthur rode back to where Gawain waited with the monstrous Ragnell. They returned to the castle in silence. Only the grotesque Lady Ragnell seemed in good spirits.

The news spread quickly throughout the castle. Gawain, the finest knight in the land, was to marry this monstrous creature! Some tittered and laughed at the spectacle; others said the Lady Ragnell must possess very great lands and estates; but mostly there was stunned silence.

Arthur took his nephew aside nervously. "Must you go through with it at once? A postponement perhaps?"

Gawain looked at him steadily. "I gave my promise, my lord. The Lady Ragnell's answer saved your life. Would you have me—"

"Your loyalty makes me ashamed! Of course you cannot break your word." And Arthur turned away.

The marriage took place in the abbey. Afterward, with Gawain and the Lady Ragnell sitting at the high dais table beside the king and queen, the strange wedding feast began.

"She takes the space of two women on the chair," muttered the knight Gareth. "Poor Gawain!"

"I would not marry such a creature for all the land in Christendom!" answered his companion.

An uneasy silence settled on the hall. Only the monstrous Lady Ragnell displayed good spirits and good appetite. Throughout the long day and evening, Gawain remained pleasant and courteous. In no way did his manner toward his strange bride show anything other than kind attention.

The wedding feast drew to a close. Gawain and his bride were conducted to their chamber and were at last alone.

The Lady Ragnell gazed at her husband thoughtfully.

"You have kept your promise well and faithfully," she observed.

Gawain inclined his head. "I could not do less, my lady."

"You've shown neither revulsion nor pity," she said. After a pause she went on, "Come now, we are wedded! I am waiting to be kissed."

Gawain went to her at once and kissed her.

71

When he stepped back, there stood before him a slender young woman with gray eyes and a serene, smiling face.

His scalp tingled in shock. "What manner of sorcery is this?" he cried hoarsely.

"Do you prefer me in this form?" she smiled and turned slowly in a full circle.

But Gawain backed away warily. "I . . . yes . . . of course . . . but . . . I don't understand . . ." For this sudden evidence of sorcery, with its unknown powers, made him confused and uneasy.

"My stepbrother, Sir Gromer, had always hated me," said the Lady Ragnell. "Unfortunately, through his mother, he has a knowledge of sorcery, and so he changed me into a monstrous creature. He said I must live in that shape until I could persuade the greatest knight in Britain to willingly choose me for his bride. He said it would be an impossible condition to meet!"

"Why did he hate you so cruelly?"

Her lips curled in amusement. "He thought me bold and unwomanly because I defied him. I refused his commands both for my property and my person."

Gawain said with admiration, "You won the 'impossible' condition he set, and now his evil spell is broken!"

"Only in part." Her clear gray eyes held his. "You have a choice, my dear Gawain, which way I will be. Would you have me in this, my own shape, at night and my former ugly shape by day? Or would you have me grotesque at night in our chamber, and my own shape in the castle by day? Think carefully before you choose."

Gawain was silent only a moment. He knelt before her and touched her hand.

"It is a choice I cannot make, my dear Ragnell. It concerns you. Whatever you choose to be—fair by day or fair by night—I will willingly abide by it."

Ragnell released a long, deep breath. The radiance in her face overwhelmed him.

"You have answered well, dearest Gawain, for your answer has broken Gromer's evil spell completely. The last condition he set has been met! For he said that if, after marriage to the greatest knight in Britain, my husband freely gave me the power of choice, the power to exercise my own free will, the wicked enchantment would be broken forever."

Thus, in wonder and in joy, began the marriage of Gawain and the Lady Ragnell.

*This story is drawn from fourteenth- and fifteenth-century tales.
Sir Gawain is a main figure in many of the stories of King Arthur
that were popular in medieval England, but particularly in northern British folklore, he is depicted as a truly just and ideal hero. A
more recent edition of the tale is* Middle English Verse Romances,
edited by **DONALD SANDS** *(1966).*

The
MONKEY'S
HEART

There once was a small gray monkey who came every day at sunrise to a large tree that grew near the sea. This tree grew so close to the edge of the sea that some of its branches hung out over the water. The tree bore a sweet, red fruit, and the monkey swung herself from branch to branch, eating her fill.

One day, as the monkey sat eating the red berries, she saw a shark swimming in the sea below her. The shark was watching the monkey with greedy eyes.

"Hello, friend," called the monkey. "Would you like a berry?"

"I was hoping you would ask," said the shark. "I would love to have some berries. I'm very tired of eating fish. They taste so salty."

"I don't care much for salty food myself," said

the monkey. She pulled off a berry and threw it down to the shark.

The first red berry hit the shark on the nose. So the shark rolled over on his back and opened his big jaws. It was quite easy then to throw the berries right into his mouth.

"Thank you! Thank you!" cried the shark. "I never ate anything that tasted so good! Would you throw down more?"

The monkey did so. And every morning after that, the shark waited underneath the tree. The monkey picked the red berries and shared them with the shark.

"You are so kind and generous," said the shark one day. "I wish I could do something for you."

"I can't think of anything," said the monkey. "I'm not fond of fish."

The shark began to tell the monkey of the wonders of the sea, of all the strange creatures who lived there. He told her of strange, faraway lands one could visit. "I could show you many new, interesting things if you'd come with me," said the shark.

The monkey was not at all sure she wanted to travel. "I would get all wet," she said, "and I do hate the water."

"You wouldn't get wet at all," cried the shark. "You could ride on my back quite safely. I will take you to visit the king of my country."

"In that case," said the monkey, "I'd be very glad to go with you."

The monkey dropped down from the tree and landed neatly on the shark's back. True to his word, the shark swam off carefully, and the monkey didn't get a bit wet.

The monkey was delighted with the ride. After they had traveled a few hours, the shark said, "Oh, I forgot to tell you! The king of my country is very ill. The only thing that will cure him is a monkey's heart."

The monkey sat very still. Then she said lightly, "That *is* too bad. I'm sorry for your king, but you should have told me this before we started out."

"It's a small matter," said the shark. "I just forgot about it."

"You see, I have no heart with me," said the monkey. "I left it behind."

"What do you mean, you have no heart?" cried the shark.

"Monkeys always leave their hearts at home when they travel," said she. "Before we set off, I took mine out and hung it on a branch of the berry tree."

"What a silly thing to do!" said the shark crossly. "You should not travel without your heart. I'll take you back at once so you can get it."

"It does seem like a lot of trouble for you," said

the monkey. "But perhaps you're right; we had better go back for it."

"No trouble at all!" said the shark. Turning around, he swam back so fast that they were back at the tree in an hour.

At once the monkey caught a low-hanging branch and swung up into the tree. In a moment she was high and safe among the leaves. Curling up, she happily went to sleep.

The shark swam round and round under the tree as he waited. At last he called out loudly, "Where are you?"

The monkey woke up and saw that the shark was still there.

"I'm up here taking a nap," she called back.

"Have you got your heart? It's time we were going."

"Going where?" asked the monkey.

"We're going to my country with your heart. Have you forgotten?"

The monkey laughed. "You must be crazy! Do you take me for a silly donkey?"

"Don't talk nonsense," said the shark. "Come down at once, or we may be too late to save the king's life."

"I'm not coming down to travel with you," said the monkey. "Only a silly donkey would do *that* twice!"

The shark thought about that for a moment. Then he said, "Perhaps a donkey's heart will do." (For he was not sure what a donkey was.) "Where will I find a silly donkey?"

"I can't tell you that," said the monkey, "but I can tell you what happened to the washerman's silly donkey."

And this is the story she told:

A washerman lived in a small house close to a great forest. With him lived a donkey who carried the man's baskets back and forth to the village nearby. The donkey finally grew bored with this life, so he ran away deep into the woods. There he lived very well on grass and nuts. With nothing to do all day, he grew fatter and fatter.

One day a hare passing by saw the fat donkey sleeping on a bed of leaves. Farther on, she passed a lion's den. The lion was quite weak and thin, for she had been sick.

The hare stopped a safe distance away. "How are you feeling today?" asked the hare politely.

"Much better," answered the lion. "But I am still too weak to get up and hunt."

"There is a nice fat donkey not far from here," said the hare.

"Why tell me that?" said the lion crossly. "You know I'm too weak to go after it. And I am very hungry!"

"Perhaps I could bring the donkey to you," said the hare.

"If you could do that," said the lion in surprise, "I would be your friend for life!"

The hare hopped back to the donkey.

"Good morning," said the hare. "I have some very good news for you."

"Really?" said the donkey. "How kind you are! What is this news?"

"My friend the lion has heard how handsome and clever and charming you are. She is quite in love with you and would like you to come visit her."

The donkey wiggled his ears in pleasure. "Where is this lovely lion?"

"She has been very ill; she is still too weak to walk. But I can take you to her."

The donkey stood up and shook the leaves from his coat. "Yes, of course I will come. Such an honor! I suppose that if we marry, I shall be king of the beasts?"

The hare didn't answer. She laughed to herself as she ran ahead to lead the donkey to the lion's den. When they arrived, the lion was sitting up, looking pale and thin.

"I'm so glad to see you," said the lion. "Please come in."

The hare said she had other things to do, and hurried away. But the donkey went into the lion's den.

"Ahem," said the donkey, swishing his tail. "Hare told me you have fallen in love with—" He stopped short in surprise and terror. The lion was crouched in the corner and her eyes were blazing. With a loud roar she leaped at the donkey.

The donkey jumped to one side just in time. He gave her a sharp kick in the ribs. The lion rolled over, clawing the donkey; the donkey bit the lion on the shoulder. Then the lion sprang at him with open jaws, but the donkey rolled over, and with another sharp kick, he knocked the lion across the den. Scrambling to his feet, he ran off into the forest.

Two or three weeks passed. The donkey's scars healed, and the lion was now strong and well.

One day the little hare stopped a safe distance from the cave and called out, "I see you are quite well again."

"Yes, indeed," said the lion. "But you promised me a donkey for my dinner, and all I got was bites and kicks. If I could get hold of that donkey, I'd tear him to pieces!"

"Yes, yes, I did promise you a donkey," said the hare. "Shall I try to bring him back here to you?"

"Do that, and I will be your friend for life," said the lion.

The hare hurried off. This time the donkey was quite far away; but the hare found him at last, rolling in moss to scratch his back.

"Good morning," said the hare. "I see your coat is as handsome as ever! The lion sent me to find you. She would like you to come see her again."

"Again!" cried the donkey as he stood up. "I don't know if I will. Last time she scratched me badly. I was very frightened."

"She was only trying to kiss you," said the hare. "But you kicked her and bit her. That made her angry."

"Oh, I see," said the silly donkey. "Are you sure?"

"Lions are like that," said the hare. "Come along and at least talk to her."

So the silly donkey once more followed the hare through the forest. This time the lion sat hidden behind a tree. When the donkey passed, she leaped out and, with a blow of her paw, knocked him dead.

"Is that the end of the story?" asked the shark.

"That's the end," said the monkey.

And the shark swam away, saying to himself, "I wish I had found a silly donkey instead of a clever monkey!"

"The Monkey's Heart" is a Swahili fairy tale. Swahili fairy and folktales often use animals to tell a moral of good and evil. This version was adopted and retold in **ANDREW LANG***'s* The Lilac Fairy Book *(1910).*

The TWELVE HUNTSMEN

A long time ago, in the forests of the Rhineland, there lived a wealthy nobleman with his daughter, Katrine. He had no son; Katrine was his only child, and from an early age she had ridden out to hunt with her father. He had taught her not only to shoot an arrow straight and true but also all the skills of hunting. When the Lady Katrine reached the usual age for marriage, many suitors came to her father's castle. However, Katrine was well content with her life. She said she had no interest in marriage, and the suitors were refused.

Then one day a young prince, Wilhelm, traveling leisurely through the country, came to stay at the nobleman's castle. As his visit lengthened from weeks into months, Katrine and the young prince fell in love. The betrothal followed, and the prince gave Katrine his ring.

Not long after this, a messenger arrived seeking the prince. Wilhelm's father, the king, was very ill, and requested his son come to him at once. The young man bade farewell to Katrine, promising to return as soon as he could.

When the young prince arrived at his distant kingdom, he found his father close to death. On his deathbed, the king demanded his son promise to marry a princess of a neighboring kingdom, for this union of the two kingdoms had long been the king's wish. He had already arranged the match with the father of the princess.

Wilhelm tried to tell his father he had made another choice. But so great was his grief at his father's suffering that he at last promised to do as his father wished. Very soon after this the father died, and the young prince became king.

Now, on the grounds of the castle, the old king had kept a lion much noted for his wisdom. One day the lion said to the grieving Wilhelm, "Do not be in a hurry to marry the princess. Postpone the marriage until the end of the year's mourning period." This suited the new king very well, and he took the lion's advice.

Although the Lady Katrine eagerly looked forward to the prince's return, she waited quite patiently for some time. There were the maids of honor to select, and plans to be made for a splendid wedding. But when months passed with no word from Wilhelm, she became hurt and then angry.

"He has forgotten me so quickly!" she exclaimed bitterly to her father. "He was not worth my love!"

Wishing to reassure his daughter, her father said, "The prince Wilhelm may have had an accident or fallen ill."

This possibility made her so silent with grief that her father said, "Have patience, my dear. If we hear nothing at the end of a year, I will send a messenger to his father's kingdom. Now tell me what you would like to make you happy, and I will give it to you."

"I can no longer be merry or patient, Father. I wish to know the truth. If the prince no longer loves me, I will forget him. But if he lies ill, I must go to him."

For a few days she considered how she could best learn the truth of the matter. The plan she formed was simple. The eleven maids of honor she had chosen were her friends and companions. Like herself, they were young and very capable horsewomen.

"I will take my eleven companions to the prince's kingdom in disguise as huntsmen," she told her father. "In that way I can learn for myself whether my betrothed is false or true."

While the green hunting clothes were cut and

sewn, the twelve maidens practiced the duties of huntsmen under the chief forester. At last the day came when the twelve companions, their long hair cut short, left the castle dressed as huntsmen. They rode through the forest and mountain passes to the distant kingdom of the prince.

As soon as they arrived in the kingdom, Katrine learned from a shepherd that the prince Wilhelm was now king and in good health, although sad and quiet since the death of his father. Katrine rode grimly on with her eleven huntsmen until they arrived at the king's castle.

Katrine's request for an audience with the king was granted. Standing proudly in the king's chamber with her eleven huntsmen, she asked that the king take them into his service. The trim, handsome appearance of the twelve green-clad youths captured the king's interest. He did not recognize the Lady Katrine at all, but he agreed to employ the twelve huntsmen.

They had not been in service at the castle very long before they heard talk that the king was expected to marry a princess from a nearby kingdom when the mourning period was ended.

Katrine's first thought was to return at once to her own country. She said to her companions, "So this is the truth of the matter! He has forgotten our betrothal and plans to wed another!"

"Let us stay longer," they counseled. "It is said the king is bound by a promise to his dying father. Do not believe the worst of Wilhelm until you are sure he does indeed prefer another to you."

Katrine agreed to this, and the twelve huntsmen continued in the king's service.

One day the old lion said to the king, "Your twelve huntsmen are not men; they are women."

"That is absurd!" said the king. "Of course they are men!"

"Test them and see. Spread peas on the floor where they will walk. Women walk lightly and will scatter the peas. Men tread firmly and will crush them."

The king followed the lion's advice. He had peas scattered on the floor of his chamber before he summoned the huntsmen. But Katrine and her maidens had trained themselves to walk as men. They trod firmly on the peas, crushing them beneath their boots.

"You are wrong," said the king to the lion. "I tested them and they are men."

"I know they are women," said the lion. "Have spinning wheels brought to the hall or antechamber they must pass through. Women always look at spinning wheels with eager interest. Men never notice them."

The spinning wheels were set up in the king's

antechamber. But when the huntsmen were again summoned, they walked past and not one glanced at the spinning wheels.

"It is clear you are wrong," said the king to the lion. "The huntsmen showed no interest at all in the spinning wheels." He decided the lion was old and foolish.

"One more test, with bows," said the lion. "Women cannot shoot an arrow as men can."

"They handle their bows as well as any huntsmen," said the king crossly. "I'll have no more of your foolish advice."

The lion turned away sulkily and lay down.

Shortly after this, a messenger came to the king with word that the princess in the nearby kingdom was growing impatient with the delay. She would arrive within a few weeks, accompanied by her father and attendants, to celebrate her betrothal to the king.

Katrine noticed that the king expressed no pleasure over this news. His face was sad with grief. When Katrine saw him pacing in the garden, sighing with despair, her heart softened.

Then the king left the garden abruptly, called for his horse, and rode recklessly away at a gallop. Katrine saddled her horse and followed him.

After riding some distance into the forest, she

came upon the king's horse, which was riderless. Cold with fear, she rode on carefully, searching this way and that until she came upon the king, lying injured by his fall.

"Thank God you've found me, huntsman!" he called. "My leg is broken, and I thought I would lie here alone tonight to be eaten by wolves."

Katrine dismounted and hurried to him. "I followed you, sire, when I saw you ride out alone."

"I am grateful, huntsman. I promise that your devotion and loyalty will be well rewarded!"

"Promise, sire? Do kings keep promises?"

The king stared at his huntsman in surprise. "A king's word is always kept!" he exclaimed. "Were it not for my promise to my father, I would not be in such despair now!"

Katrine pulled off her gloves to care for his injury. "Does a king break one promise to keep another?"

But the king did not answer. He was staring at the ring on the huntsman's finger. "Where did you get that ring? Did the Lady Katrine send you?"

"The ring was given to me with the promise of a prince," said Katrine.

At this, the king looked into her eyes and knew her. But his great joy at this discovery gave way almost at once to despair.

"How can I break my promise to my father, given

when he lay on his deathbed? I have delayed as long as I could, but the princess grows impatient."

"Such a promise cannot be binding when you were already betrothed to me!" said Katrine. "Since your father valued the lion's wisdom, why don't you ask him for advice?"

The king agreed to this. "The old fellow is not so foolish after all—for he was right about you and your huntsmen!"

After the king, his injured leg bound with branches, was carried back to the castle on a litter, he had the lion brought to him. When the lion said that the king's betrothal to Katrine overrode the promise he had given his father, the king's last scruple was dissolved.

The king's ministers were sent to explain the situation to the princess, and very soon afterward the wedding of the king and the Lady Katrine was celebrated with great joy and feasting throughout the kingdom.

"The Twelve Huntsmen" is a German fairy tale originally included in Grimms' Fairy Tales. *This version has been adapted from* The Green Fairy Book *(1892), edited by* **ANDREW LANG**.

There once was a farmer who went out with his oxen one morning to plow his field.

He had just finished plowing one row when a tiger walked up to him and said, "Good morning, friend. How are you today?"

"Good morning, sir. I am very well, sir," said the farmer. He was shaking with fear, but he felt it wise to be polite.

"I see you have two fine oxen," said the tiger. "I am very hungry. Take off their yokes at once, please, for I intend to eat them."

The farmer's courage returned now that he realized the tiger did not plan to eat *him*. Still, he did not want to give up his oxen for the tiger's meal.

"My friend," said the farmer, "I need these oxen to plow my field. Surely a brave tiger like you can hunt for a good meal elsewhere!"

"Never mind that!" said the tiger crossly. "Unyoke the oxen. I will be ready to eat them in a moment." And the tiger began to sharpen his teeth and claws on a stone.

"The oxen are very tough and will be hard to eat," pleaded the farmer. "My wife has a fat young milk cow at home. Spare my oxen and I'll bring you the cow."

The tiger agreed to this. He thought a tender young cow would make a much easier meal for him than tough oxen. So he said, "Very well. I will wait here in the field while you go home and get the cow. But bring the cow back as quickly as you can. I'm very hungry.

The farmer took the oxen and went sadly homeward.

"Why do you come home so early in the day?" called his wife. "It is not time for dinner!"

"A tiger came into the field and wanted to eat the oxen," said the farmer. "But I told him he could have the cow instead. Now I must bring him the cow."

"What!" she cried. "You would save your old oxen and give him my beautiful cow? Where will our children get milk? And how can I cook our food without butter?"

"We'll have no food at all unless I plow the field for my crops," said the farmer crossly. "Now untie the cow for me."

"No, I will not give up my cow to the tiger!" said his wife. "Surely you can think of a better way to get rid of the tiger!"

"No, I cannot. He is sitting in my field waiting for me, and he's very hungry."

His wife thought a moment. Then she said, "Go back to the tiger and tell him your wife is bringing the cow. Leave the rest to me."

The farmer did not want to go back to the tiger without the cow. But he had no better idea, so he walked slowly back to the field.

"Where is the cow?" roared the tiger angrily.

"My wife will bring the cow very soon," said the farmer.

At this, the tiger began to prowl about, growling and lashing his tail. The poor farmer's knees shook in terror.

In the meantime, his wife dressed herself in her husband's best clothes. She tied the turban very high on her head to make her look very tall. She took a long knife from the kitchen and put it into her belt. Then she put a saddle on their pony and rode off to the field.

As she drew near, she called out to her husband in a loud voice, "My good man, are there any tigers about? I've been hunting tiger for two days, and I'm hungry for tiger meat!" And she slashed the air above her head with the knife in a very threatening way.

The farmer was so surprised he could not answer.

"Aha!" cried his wife. "Is that a tiger I see hiding in the grass? I ate three tigers for breakfast the other day, and now I'm hungry for more!" And she started to ride toward the tiger.

These words frightened the tiger. He turned tail and bolted into the forest. He ran so fast he knocked over a jackal who was sitting and waiting to feast on the ox bones after the tiger had finished his meal.

"Why are you running away?" called the jackal.

"Run! Run for your life!" cried the tiger. "There is a terribly fierce horseman back in the field! He thinks nothing of eating three tigers for breakfast."

"That was no horseman," laughed the jackal. "That was only the farmer's wife dressed up as a hunter."

The tiger came back slowly. "Are you sure?"

"Did the sun get in your eyes? Didn't you see

her hair hanging down from the turban?" asked the jackal impatiently.

The tiger was still doubtful. "He looked like a hunter, and he swung that big knife as if he were going to kill me!"

"Don't give up your meal so easily," cried the brave jackal. "Go back to the field. I will follow and wait in the grass."

The tiger did not like that idea at all. "I think you want me to be killed!"

"No, of course not," said the jackal. He was hungry and impatient. "If you like, we will go together, side by side."

The tiger was still suspicious of the jackal's motives. "You may run away and leave me after we get there."

"We can tie our tails together," said the jackal. "Then I can't run away."

The tiger thought this a good idea. So they tied their tails together in a strong knot, and set off together for the field.

The farmer and his wife were still in the field, laughing over the trick she had played on the tiger. Suddenly they saw the tiger and the jackal trotting toward them with their tails tied together.

The farmer shouted to his wife, "Now the tiger has a jackal with him. Come away! Hurry!"

The wife said no, she would not. She waited until

the tiger and jackal were near. Then she called out, "Dear Mr. Jackal, how very kind of you to bring me such a nice fat tiger to eat. After I eat my fill, you can have the bones."

When the tiger heard this, he became wild with terror. He forgot the jackal, and he forgot the knot in their tails. He leaped for the tall grass. Then off he ran, dragging the jackal behind him over stones and through thorn bushes.

The jackal howled and cried for the tiger to stop. But the howls behind him only scared the tiger more, and he ran on until they both collapsed in a heap, more dead than alive.

As for the farmer, he was very proud of his wife's clever trick—for the tiger never came back to their field again.

This telling of "The Tiger and the Jackal" comes from Tales of the Punjab *(1917), edited by* **FLORA ANNIE STEEL**. *The story itself has over one hundred versions featuring different animals including a crocodile, a snake, and a wolf. The original tale can be dated back to versions in the* Panchatantra, *an ancient Indian collection of animal fables.*

EAST of the SUN, WEST of the MOON

Once upon a time, a poor woodcutter and his wife lived in the forest. They had so many children that they could scarcely feed and clothe them. They were all fine children, but the bravest and most cheerful was the eldest daughter.

One evening late in the year, when the cold wind blew hard against their little cottage, they heard a loud knock on the door. The father got up from the hearth and went outside to see who it was. A large white bear stood outside the door, waiting for him.

"Good evening to you," said the White Bear.

"Good evening," said the woodcutter politely.

"I've taken a fancy to your eldest daughter," said the White Bear. "If she will come away to live with me, I can promise your family prosperity and good fortune."

"No, indeed!" said the woodcutter. "I'd rather

stay as poor as we are than let my daughter go off to live with a bear."

The White Bear looked at him sadly. "Perhaps you will change your mind. I'll return next week."

But the woodcutter shook his head and closed the door.

The eldest daughter, who had been standing near the open door, had heard the Bear's words. She thought the White Bear had a gentle, kind manner; he did not seem at all fierce.

The lass thought about the Bear's request for several days. She made up her mind that when the Bear came back, she would go off with him, and neither her father nor her mother could talk her out of it.

When the Bear returned in exactly one week, the lass answered his knock and said she was ready to go with him. She said farewell to her family, climbed onto his shaggy back, and off they went.

"Are you afraid?" asked the White Bear.

"No, not at all," said the lass.

"There is nothing to fear," said the White Bear. "Hold tight to my fur and you won't fall off."

They traveled this way for a long time, until at last they came to a steep cliff. The White Bear knocked on the rocky face of the cliff, and a door opened for them.

Inside was a fine castle of many rooms, all brightly lit and richly furnished. The Bear led the way to a room where a table was laid with supper waiting. Then he gave the lass a small silver bell. Whenever she wanted anything, said the Bear, she was to ring the bell, and it would be brought to her. The lass thanked him, and the Bear left.

The lass was very hungry, so she ate the supper. Then, very sleepy from her long journey, she found a bedchamber and went to sleep.

She lived cheerfully in the castle under the hill for some months. Her only companion all this time was the White Bear, and as time went on she became quite fond of him. But although he talked with her quite gaily, he would answer no questions about either the castle or himself.

Only one thing troubled her. At night, just as she was falling asleep, she would hear someone come into the room and lie down. In the morning, when she awoke, there was no one to be seen. She puzzled over this for some time, wondering if it was the White Bear who came into the room—or perhaps a strange underground creature of some kind.

She grew silent thinking about it. The White

Bear, noticing her silence, said, "Lass, this castle and all that is in it are yours. I wish you could be happy here! The silver bell will bring you anything you want. Ask me no questions, trust me, and nothing shall harm you."

"I do trust you," said the lass.

"Are you tired of my company?" asked the White Bear sadly. "Do you wish me to go away?"

"No," said the lass warmly. "I have become very fond of you."

But she became more and more curious about the creature who came into her room at night. Since she could ask no questions, she resolved to find out for herself.

The next night she stayed awake until she heard the creature come into the room and fall deeply asleep. Then she got up and lit a candle.

When she brought the candle over to gaze down at the sleeping figure, she could scarcely believe her eyes! It was a young man with fair hair and a pleasant, open face. As she gazed in surprise, three drops of hot tallow fell from the candle onto his white shirt. The young man woke up.

He stared at her in sorrow. "Oh, lass, what you have done will bring grief to us both! A wicked troll has bewitched me so that I am a white bear by day and a man by night. There is only one way for me to break the enchantment. If you had willingly stayed with me a full year without knowing my true form, I would be freed. Now that you have seen me, I am still in their power."

"Surely there is something I can do to save you?" cried the lass.

He shook his head. "I must leave you now to return to the Land of the Trolls."

"Can I come with you?" she asked. "I am not afraid."

But again he shook his head.

"Tell me the way, then, and I will search for you until I find you."

He looked at her with gratitude and love. "I'm afraid you will never find that place. Few mortals can. It lies East of the Sun and West of the Moon, and there is no road that leads to it."

Before he could say anything more, both the man and the castle disappeared. The lass found herself sitting in the middle of a forest, dressed in the ragged clothes she had worn when she first met the White Bear.

"I failed to help the White Bear break the enchantment," she thought, "but if I seek him out in the Land of the Trolls I may be able to help him escape their power."

So she started off and walked many weary days,

asking everyone she met, "Can you tell me the way to the place that lies East of the Sun and West of the Moon?"

But no one had ever heard of the place until one day she met an old woman who said kindly, "I have heard a prince is held prisoner in a castle that lies East of the Sun and West of the Moon. How to get there I do not know. Ask the East Wind."

The lass walked and walked until she reached the home of the East Wind. There she asked if the East Wind knew the way to the castle East of the Sun, West of the Moon.

"I have heard of it," said the East Wind, "but I don't know the way. I have never blown so far. Perhaps the West Wind knows. I will carry you there, lass."

With a gentle swoop she was lifted up into the air and carried along over the earth to the home of the West Wind.

"This lass seeks the prince in the castle East of the Sun and West of the Moon," said the East Wind. "Do you know where it is?"

"No," said the West Wind, "I have never blown that far. I will take her to the South Wind, who has traveled over more lands than we have."

With a brisk flurry, the West Wind took her up into the clouds and carried her along swiftly.

"Are you afraid?" called the West Wind.

"Not at all," said the lass.

When at last they reached the home of the South Wind, the West Wind told of the lass's quest.

"I've blown over many lands," said the South Wind, "but I've not seen such a place. I'll take the lass to the North Wind. The North Wind is the oldest and strongest of us. If the North Wind does not know where it is, it cannot be found!"

The South Wind lifted her high above the earth and carried her along on a strong, steady breeze until they reached the cold home of the North Wind.

"What do you want?" roared the North Wind.

"You needn't be so cross!" said the South Wind. "I have a brave lass here who seeks the prince in the castle East of the Sun, West of the Moon. Have you ever been there?"

"I know where it is," said the North Wind. "It's a great distance. I blew an aspen leaf there once, and I was so tired I had to rest before I could return."

"Can you tell me the way?" asked the lass. "I will go myself."

"No need for that," growled the North Wind. "If you are not afraid to come with me, I'll carry you there."

"I'm not afraid," said the lass. "I will go with you, thank you, for I must get there as fast as I can."

The North Wind blew hard, and with a roar they

shot up into the air high above the land and the seas. They raced along, the North Wind blowing with all its power. Down below, a storm raged. Trees were uprooted, and on the sea, ships tossed madly. They tore on and on over the sea, until even the powerful North Wind became weaker and weaker. They dropped down lower and lower over the crests of the waves. The icy spray splashed her legs.

"Are you afraid?" puffed the North Wind.

"No, I am not afraid," she replied. But she was glad to see the outline of land ahead.

With a final burst of strength, the North Wind dropped her on the shore close to the castle that lay East of the Sun and West of the Moon.

"I must rest a day on the shore," puffed the North Wind faintly. "This is no place for a lass. Are you sure you want to stay?"

The lass said she must free the prince if she can. So she thanked the North Wind and went on her way.

Since it was still daylight, there was not a troll to be seen. She walked to the castle and sat down near the gates to think of how she could free the prince.

As soon as the sun went down, out came the trolls: hairy, red-eyed creatures scurrying about chattering and shrieking to one another in great excitement. The sight of them was enough to scare the bravest mortal.

But the lass had come this far in her quest, and she would not hesitate now. Gathering her courage, she boldly walked up to one of the troll women.

"Can you tell me what is going on?" she asked politely. "Is there some work I could do for a night's lodging and a bit of food?"

"Tonight is the night the prince must choose a bride from among us!" cried the troll woman exultantly. "When the moon stands high over the tree-tops, we meet in that clearing by the old oak—and the one who can wash the three spots of tallow from his shirt can claim the prince!"

The troll woman shrieked with glee as she hurried off after the others. Trolls were coming to the clearing from all directions, so the lass followed them.

In the clearing was a large pot of water, and in front of it sat rows of chattering trolls. When the moon stood high above the treetops, the prince came with his shirt. He looked at the throng of trolls and grew pale. But when he saw the lass standing alone at the rear of the crowd, he smiled in relief.

"Now we'll begin," said a troll woman who seemed to be their leader. And she began, very confidently, to wash the shirt. But the more she rubbed and scrubbed, the bigger the spots grew.

"Ha!" cried another troll woman. "It's clear you cannot wash the shirt clean. You can never claim the prince. Let me try!"

She seized the shirt and went to work. But she did no better. Her scrubbing and rubbing only made the spots bigger and darker.

All the trolls clamored to wash the shirt. They took turns, grabbing it from one another, each troll scrubbing away with her claws as hard as she could. The shirt only looked darker and dirtier than ever; the three tallow spots did not come out. By now the night was ending.

"You have all tried, and none of you can wash the tallow spots off!" cried the prince. "I see a beggar lass standing there. I'm sure she knows how to wash the shirt! Come here, lass," he called.

The lass went to him quickly.

"Can you wash the shirt clean?" he asked.

"I don't know," she said. "I can try."

She took the shirt to the large cauldron of water and dipped the shirt down into it. At once the shirt became clean and white. When she took it out of the water, the tallow spots were gone.

"Yes," said the prince, smiling, "that proves you are the lass for me!"

The pack of trolls shrieked in disappointed rage.

They scrambled to their feet to attack, but the prince clasped hands with the lass and ran for the shore.

At that moment the sun came up. The trolls, trapped by daylight, turned to stone, where they stand to this day.

As for the prince and the lass—the North Wind, with a strong gust, lifted them high above the sea and carried them back to their own country.

"East of the Sun, West of the Moon" is a Norwegian fairy tale, collected and recorded in Popular Tales from the Norse *(1859), by* **PETER CHRISTEN ASBJØRNSEN** *and* **JØRGEN MOE**. *The story is related to both "The Tale of Cupid and Psyche" from* The Golden Ass *and the French tale "Beauty and the Beast."*

The GIANT'S DAUGHTER

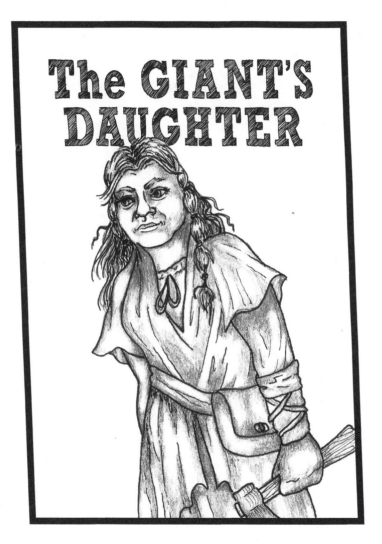

A long time ago, giants and trolls dwelled in the high mountain forests above the northern fjords. They kept to themselves and had little to do with the people who lived in the valley below—except to scare the wits out of one of them now and then.

Gina was different; she was quite curious about the humans living in the little houses down in the valley and along the shore. Of course she was still young, as giants go, and not fully grown. That would explain her foolishness, thought her father.

"She has the curiosity of a bear cub," grumbled her mother, "but it's very unnatural to bother with humankind."

"Have nothing to do with people," advised the elder giants. "Small, stupid creatures! Frightened by a boulder thrown or a sheep carried off!"

Nonetheless, on clear days, young Gina would sit on a rock at the lower edge of the forest, watching the people below go about their daily work. It seemed to Gina that these people had a splendid time; the maidservants especially caught her attention, moving about from dairy to stream, laughing together as they worked.

"The work is so easy, I could do it with one hand," thought she. "And so many kinds of food just for the taking!" Gina, it must be admitted, was just a little greedy. She loved to eat.

She was also quite stubborn. Once she had made up her mind to go down to the village below, no one could dissuade her.

Her cousins, the mountain trolls, shrilled, "But they are our enemy! You will be killed, and it will serve you right."

"You foolish child," cried her mother in alarm. "Mark my words, there will be trouble. No good will come of it."

"No good will come of it!" warned the uncles, the aunts, and all the rest of the giants.

But they were all quite wrong.

One day Gina, hop-skipping over the boulders, came down the mountain to the village. At the first two houses where she stopped to ask for work, she had no luck at all.

At the third house, the mistress looked at the

very tall, strongly built girl with the large round head, and thought, "Here's a bargain indeed! An odd-looking country girl, but she'll do very well for chopping wood and pounding the wash." She told Gina to come in.

Gina bent down, ducking her head to enter the house. "Such queer, tiny houses," thought she. "Doorways much too small, roofs much too low for comfort."

Gina was set to work at once, but it was not many days before the mistress regretted having taken in the strange girl. Gina chopped wood with a will, but so violently that the chunks flew in all directions—one struck a rooster stone dead; one sent a dog yowling off in surprise; another whacked a cart horse so sharply that he bolted off, spilling rounds of cheese right and left. Then she carried such huge armloads of wood into the house that the door burst off its hinges.

Set to work with a tub of wash at the stream, she pounded the laundry so thoroughly that all the clothes and linens came out in rags. To make matters worse, Gina ate more than all the other servants put together. Even between meals she found her way into the storeroom, and sat happily devouring jars of honey, vats of pickles, and long strings of sausages.

The mistress brought this tale of woe to her

husband, a merchant. "She is impossible!" cried the mistress. "We must get rid of her. When she scours pots, she grinds holes in them! When she washes dishes, she breaks half of them! If she sits on my chairs, they collapse. No, I can't keep her a day longer; she'll be the ruin of us!"

But if Gina was greedy about food, the merchant was miserly about money. "She's powerfully strong and we pay her no wages," he pointed out to his wife—for Gina knew nothing of money or wages. "We could never get a village girl to work for us without payment. And where could we find one half as strong? Gina's twice as strong as a man. I'll find work for her."

So although the mistress complained bitterly about the havoc Gina caused and wanted to get rid of her at once, the merchant insisted she be kept on.

He set Gina to heavy outdoor work, carrying bales of hay to the barn. But Gina thought it fun to toss the bales into the hayloft, and if she knocked down a farmhand in the process, she merely roared with laughter. If a horse kicked her, she gave the animal a powerful kick right back. All this caused such an uproar in the barnyard that the merchant quickly set Gina to unloading the fishing boats that came to his wharf. Here she did the work of two or three men.

Delighted with such a strong and willing worker,

the merchant used Gina everywhere—from sausage and cheese making to building a new storage barn. In the new barn he had Gina build a room and bed of her own, for the mistress declared that she was not fit to live in a house. The merchant, however, rubbed his hands in satisfaction thinking of the money he saved.

And what about Gina? Gina was enjoying herself. The heavy work did not bother her at all. She joined in the village dances, but she swung her partners with such vigor that they whirled away across the field. After that, partners were hard to find. Still, everything new fascinated her. Although she thought humans most peculiar in their ways, she marveled at their cleverness.

Their houses were too small, their furniture too flimsy, but it was fine to sleep on a bed instead of a pile of leaves, or use an ax to chop wood instead of breaking it apart with her hands. And to think one might keep chickens to have eggs whenever one wished! Her sharp, inquisitive eyes took in everything that went on around her.

Things went on this way for several months. But while the merchant became more and more pleased with his bargain, the mistress became more and more irritated with Gina. She determined to get rid of her.

In the spring, the merchant prepared to sail down

125

to Bergen on a trading voyage. His wife announced she would go with him. Just before they set sail, she took Gina aside and said sharply, "I don't want to find you here when we return. I advise you to go back to wherever you came from!"

Then she quickly joined her husband aboard the ship, and they sailed away down the fjord with a stiff breeze. Gina was left on shore with the village folk who had turned out to see the merchant off. Next to her stood two maidservants from the village.

"Wish you were going with them?" said one. "Save the money they pay you, Gina, and you can go to Bergen yourself someday!"

"Money they pay me?" repeated Gina in surprise.

"Your wages for working," said the other. "I noticed you never spend any money. You must have a nice little sum hidden away!"

"They never gave me any money for working!"

The two girls laughed at her. "Oh you *are* a green one! You worked almost a year for nothing?"

"Greedy old man," said the other. "No wonder he's so rich!"

When Gina finally understood that all the other country girls were paid, her eyes became quite red with anger. She stalked back to the merchant's place. There she sat down and thought for a long time.

"Payment I shall have," she said finally. "I'll take it myself!"

At once she set to work. She pulled an old cart out from the barn and loaded it with all the things she had decided to take with her. In went a cock and a hen, an ax, nails—she knew what she needed for the success of her plan. And when the cart was filled, she didn't forget to toss in a round wheel of cheese, a crock of pickles, and several strings of her favorite sausages.

Then she pulled the loaded cart up the mountain until she reached the high pine forests, the land of the trolls and giants.

Swinging the ax with gusto, she soon converted trees into the framework of a tall one-room house. She made sure that the doorway was big and wide, and the roof high enough for a full-grown giant. Next to it was a fenced-in yard for the cock and hen.

From time to time, the giants and trolls came by to watch her work and to gape in astonishment at so much mad activity.

"Poor Gina," they said to each other. "She's become as crazy as a loon, living with humans all that time. I knew no good would come of it!"

"She'll never marry now," lamented Gina's mother. "She's collected no fur pelts for dowry. What sensible giant would want that pile of wood?"

But again they were all quite wrong.

When Gina had finished all her work, the first frost sparkled on the ground, and the smell of snow was in the air. She now had a tall house made of logs, snug against the winter cold. She had an open hearth and a stack of firewood; a big, solid chair; a large bed covered with fur pelts; chickens safely housed in a lean-to; rounds of cheese made from wild goat and reindeer milk; and sausages and wild boar hams hanging from the rafters.

By the time the heavy snow had settled on the mountain, even the sour trolls had to admit that the warm log house was better than a cave or a deep underground hole. It dawned on the folk of the forest that Gina was not crazy at all. She was in fact very clever.

And what better dowry could a young giant girl have than a snug hut and strings of fragrant sausages? All the giant folk now called her Clever Gina, and as the winter thawed into spring, Gina was besieged with offers to marry.

"Perhaps I'll marry, or perhaps I won't," she said carelessly. "I'll think about it." And since the young giants were very eager to bring her rabbits or wild boar and other game in exchange for eggs, cheese, or the loan of her ax, it seemed to Gina that "thinking about it" was a very good arrangement indeed.

"The Giant's Daughter" has been adapted from a Norwegian tale in Weird Tales of the Northern Seas *(1903), edited by* **JONAS LIE** *and translated by* **R. NISBET BAIN**.

Long ago, long before the white people came, Canada turned very cold. In all the land there was not a flower nor a tree left alive. Snow and ice were everywhere.

This terrible cold covered the land for a long time. Because the ground was frozen, the First Nations people could not grow corn. The people were starving, and it seemed as if the whole land must perish.

Although Glooskap, the ruler of the Wabanaki people, was wise and strong, he had no power against the ice and snow covering his land. He tried all his magic, but it was of no use, for this terrible cold was caused by a powerful giant who came into the land from the Far North. His breath could wither trees; he could destroy the corn and kill man and beast.

The giant's name was Winter. He was very old and very strong, and he had ruled in the Far North long before the coming of man.

Glooskap went alone to the giant's ice tent, thinking to bribe or force the Winter Giant to go away. But even Glooskap, with all his magic power, fell under the spell of the beauty of the giant's land. In the sunlight it sparkled like crystal with pin-points of many colors. The trees, laden with snow, had strange, fantastic shapes. At night the sky was filled with flashing, quivering lights, and even the stars had a rare brilliance.

The giant told tales of ancient times when all the land was silent, white, and beautiful. Then he used his charm of slumber until Glooskap fell asleep. But Glooskap was very strong, and Winter could not kill him, even in his sleep. After he had slept for a long time, Glooskap awoke, rose, and went back to his people.

One day soon after this, his tale-bearer, Tatler the Loon, brought him good news. Far away there was a wonderful Southland where it was always warm. Ruling over this land was a queen who could easily overcome the giant—indeed, she was the only one on earth whose power the giant feared. Glooskap knew the queen could save his people. He decided he must go to the Southland to find her.

She lived, said Tatler the Loon, in the Wilderness of Flowers. And he gave Glooskap directions to find her. Glooskap traveled many miles across the land to the sea. On the shore he sang the magic song that whales obey. His old friend Blob the Whale came quickly to his call. Climbing on to her back, he sailed away.

Now, Blob the Whale had a strange rule for passengers. She said to Glooskap, "You must close your eyes tightly while I carry you. If you open them, I will go aground on a reef or sandbar and be stuck fast. Then you may be drowned." Glooskap promised to keep his eyes tightly closed.

The whale swam for many days. Each day the water grew warmer and the air grew milder. Then the soft air no longer smelled of the salt sea, but of fruit and flowers. They had left the deep sea, and were in the shallow water closer to land.

Blob the Whale now swam more cautiously.

Down in the sand the clams were singing a song of warning, telling of the sandbar beneath the water. But the whale did not understand the language of the clams. Glooskap did.

Glooskap thought it would be a good idea if the whale *did* go aground near shore. Then he could more easily walk to land. So he opened his left eye. At once the whale struck a sandbar close to the beach; Glooskap was able to leap from her head and wade ashore.

Stuck fast and fearful that she would never get free, the whale became very angry. But Glooskap put one end of his strong bow against the whale's jaw, and with a mighty push, he sent old Blob back into the deep water.

Walking far inland with great strides, Glooskap soon found the road Loon had described. It was the Rainbow Road, which led to the Wilderness of Flowers. Here the Winter Giant had no power. The winds were always warm; snow and ice were unknown.

Glooskap went quickly along the road until he came to an orange grove where the air was fragrant with blossoms. Not far ahead he saw a clearing, and from it came the sound of singing.

Creeping closer, he stood behind a tree to watch. Around the soft grass of the clearing, every

kind of flower was in bloom. Birds with brightly colored feathers fluttered and sang in the trees. He had found old Tatler the Loon's Wilderness of Flowers.

In the open space, four maidens sang a song of summer as they moved through the graceful steps of a dance. Taller and more splendid than the others was a maiden whose long brown hair was crowned with flowers. For some time Glooskap gazed in silence.

Then he noticed an old woman nearby, faded but still beautiful, also watching the dancers.

"Who are these maidens?" he asked

"The maiden with the headdress of flowers is the queen," she answered. "Her name is Summer. The maidens with her are her children: Sunshine, Light, and Flowers."

Here at last was the queen who could challenge Winter and force him to go away! Glooskap began to sing his magic songs, until he lured the Summer Queen to his side.

He spoke to her of his people, cold and hungry, of his Northland frozen and desolate under the power of Winter. "Only you can defeat the Winter Giant and save my people," he said.

The Summer Queen considered Glooskap's words. "I will come with you to save your people," she said at last. "But I cannot stay. I must return again to my Southland."

Glooskap nodded. Then, with their hands clasped together, they began the long return journey by land. He ran north with the Summer Queen for many, many days until at last they reached the Northland.

Glooskap was saddened to see his country still desolate and covered with ice. Only a few of his people remained alive—and they had fallen asleep under the Winter Giant's power.

The Summer Queen and Glooskap hurried on to the ice home of Winter. The giant welcomed them with a grin, thinking to freeze both Glooskap and the glowing queen with his power.

How splendidly she stood smiling before the giant! Winter used all his most powerful charms to numb the pair, but the queen softly sang a summer song. The charms of Winter failed.

Large drops ran down the giant's face. His ice tent slowly melted away. The Summer Queen spread her strange power until everything the Winter Giant had frozen came to life. Melted snow ran down the rivers; buds swelled again on trees; grass and corn sprang up with new life.

Angrily, the Winter Giant wept tears like cold rain, for he knew he was defeated.

The Summer Queen spoke: "I have proved that I am more powerful than you, Winter Giant, but I have no wish to destroy you. I give you all the country of the Far North for your own. You may come back to Glooskap's country every year for six months only; but when you do return here, your stay must be much less severe. When you leave in the spring, I will come from the Southland and rule in Glooskap's country for six months."

Winter bowed his head and accepted the terms—for he feared that if he did not, he would melt away entirely.

And Glooskap was pleased with the queen's generosity, for he did not wish the beauty of snow on the land to be lost forever.

The Winter Giant left at once for the Far North. There he reigns with all his power. In late autumn, when the Summer Queen returns to her homeland, the Winter Giant comes back to Glooskap's country. But at the end of six months, the Summer Queen always returns with songbirds and bright flowers to drive the Winter Giant back to his northern home.

In this way, the fair Summer Queen and the ancient Winter Giant divide the land of Canada between them.

Glooskap (other spellings include Gluskap, Glooscap) is one of the primary heroes in creation stories and legends from the Wabanaki tribes of Canada and New England. Glooskap is featured in many origin stories and tales that explain the natural world. This version of "The Summer Queen" has been adapted from Canadian Wonder Tales *(1918 and 1922) by* **CYRUS MACMILLAN**.

SUGGESTED READING

Favilli, Elena, and Francesca Cavallo. 2016. *Goodnight Stories for Rebel Girls*. San Francisco: Timbuktu Labs.

Gaiman, Neil. 2015. *The Sleeper and the Spindle*. New York: HarperCollins.

Goble, Paul. 1993. *The Girl Who Loved Wild Horses*. New York: Aladdin.

Hamilton, Virginia. 1995. *Her Stories: African American Folktales, Fairy Tales, and True Tales*. New York: Blue Sky Press.

Lansky, Bruce. 2002. *The Best of Girls to the Rescue: Girls Save the Day*. Minnetonka, MN: Meadowbrook Press.

Martin, Rafe, and David Shannon. 1998. *The Rough-Face Girl*. New York: PaperStar Books.

McGoon, Greg. 2015. *The Royal Heart.* Lakewood, CA: Avid Readers Publishing Group.

Ragan, Kathleen. 2000. *Fearless Girls, Wise Women, and Beloved Sisters: Heroines in Folktales from around the World.* New York: W. W. Norton & Company.

Sand, George. 2014. *What Flowers Say: And Other Stories.* Translated by Holly Erskine Hirko. New York: The Feminist Press.

Schatz, Kate. 2016. *Rad Women Worldwide.* Berkeley, CA: Ten Speed Press.

Yolen, Jane. 1986. *Favorite Folktales from around the World.* New York: Pantheon.

———. 2000. *Not One Damsel in Distress: World Folktales for Strong Girls.* Boston: Houghton Mifflin Harcourt.

ACKNOWLEDGMENTS

everal thousand individual folktales were read in the search for neglected tales of resourceful and courageous heroines to retell. In addition to public and university libraries, the Reference Collection of Children's Books at the Donnell Library in New York City and the Osborne and Lillian H. Smith Collections in Toronto were very useful in researching the folktales. I take this opportunity to express my thanks to the reference librarians in both Toronto and the New York area for their generous help in locating needed volumes.

ETHEL JOHNSTON PHELPS *(1914–1984) held a master's degree in medieval literature; she was coeditor of a Ricardian journal and published articles on fifteenth-century subjects. Originally from Long Island, her activities included acting, writing, and directing in radio drama and community theater. Three of her one-act plays have been produced.*

SUKI BOYNTON *is the senior graphic designer at the Feminist Press. She is a graduate of Connecticut College with a BA in art history and has a degree in graphic design from the Art Institute of Charleston, South Carolina. She currently lives in Queens.*

The Feminist Press is a nonprofit educational organization founded to amplify feminist voices. FP publishes classic and new writing from around the world, creates cutting-edge programs, and elevates silenced and marginalized voices in order to support personal transformation and social justice for all people.

See our complete list of books at
feministpress.org